LIKE THE
WILLOW
TREE

LIKE THE
WILLOW
TREE

LOIS LOWRY

A Dear America novel

SCHOLASTIC INC.

With thanks to Leonard L. Brooks, director of the Shaker Library and Museum at Sabbathday Lake; to Tina Agren, the librarian/archivist; and to Brother Arnold Hadd, who patiently and generously answered questions that he has probably answered a hundred times before.

This book was originally published by Scholastic Inc. in 2011 as part of the Dear America series.

While the events described and some of the characters in this book may be based on actual historical events and real people, Lydia Amelia Pierce is a fictional character, created by the author, and her diary and its epilogue are works of fiction.

ISBN 978-1-338-72432-5

10 9 8 7 6 5 4 3 2 1   20 21 22 23 24

Printed in the U.S.A.   40
This edition first printing 2020

Book design by Kevin Callahan and Elizabeth B. Parisi

INTRODUCTION

I wrote this book in 2010, ten years ago. I looked back into the archives, the history books, the old newspapers, and wrote about what it was like in Portland, Maine, in 1918 when the flu epidemic struck suddenly and took the lives of so many people.

The Pierce family is fictional. I made them up. But, as I always do when I write fiction, I tried to put myself into the heart and mind of the main character, eleven-year-old Lydia. How annoyed she was at first, that an illness—something that was happening to other people—was wrecking her birthday plans. Then how confused and concerned, as neighbors became ill. And finally how frightened, how grief-stricken, when it struck her own family and changed the entire course of what had been an ordinary and pleasant life.

As I write this now, in 2020, I am recalling that only four weeks ago I was annoyed because the threat of a coming epidemic had caused the cancellation of a lovely vacation, a river cruise in France, that I had planned. Within a few days, my annoyance changed to concern when people I knew became ill. Then, in a startlingly short time, three of my neighbors had died. Today, someone I love is hospitalized. A piece of fiction about a long-ago set of events seems frighteningly real.

This morning, in my house just outside Portland, Maine, I picked up *Like the Willow Tree* and re-read those first chapters. Lydia Pierce complains, on October 4, 1918, "The Portland Board of Health has issued an order suddenly that no gatherings are to be held at theaters or motion picture houses or dance halls. None at all! And schools are to be closed as well."

The same thing is true here today, over a hundred years later.

On October 6, 1918, Lydia comments that her father thinks they are making too much of it. "He intends to go to work tomorrow and every day to follow and he expects his fellow employees at the store to do the same. He thinks Mayor Clarke is a fool to have closed down a whole city."

Today, not only the city of Portland but the entire state of Maine is closed down.

On October 7th, just over a hundred years ago, Lydia describes that those few people still out and about are wearing gauze masks.

I put on a mask yesterday when I entered the grocery store.

I cringed as I read on and saw that Lydia's father leaned over the baby carriage on the back porch and kissed her sleeping baby sister. *No!* I found myself thinking. *Don't do that!*

Two days ago I lowered the window of my car in order to have a conversation with my grandson, unexpectedly home from his shut-down college, who had stopped across the road in his own car. *No closer!* we said to each other.

So we have learned *something* from 1918.

I closed the book, not wanting to read on, knowing what would too soon befall the Pierce family.

We do, I think, learn from the past. The memories are sad, and the learning can be painful. But I am also reminded, re-reading *Like the Willow Tree*, that we are resilient. That we care about and help each other, and that we emerge stronger than we ever knew we could be.

Lois Lowry
Portland, Maine, 2020

LIKE THE WILLOW TREE

PORTLAND,
MAINE

1918

Friday, October 4, 1918

I am desolate. Mother and Father had agreed that for my birthday today, they would take me (and my brother, Daniel, though I don't think it was entirely fair that Daniel should be going, since it is not *his* birthday, just mine) to the moving pictures to see Tom Mix in *Cupid's Roundup* at the Strand Theatre.

I have never been to the Strand Theatre and it has a Wurlitzer organ. And I have never seen Tom Mix, but he is King of the Cowboys and is deeply in love with the beautiful actress Victoria Forde.

I have always wished for my name to be Victoria instead of Lydia, which is as dull as dishwater. When my baby sister was born in July I hoped that we would name her Victoria, but Mother and Father thought it too fancy a name (it is a queen's name, after all, they pointed out) and so our baby is named Lucy, almost as dull as my name, Lydia.

Mrs. O'Brien, next door, said she would watch Lucy for us tonight, so that we could go to the moving pictures. It would be a much more grown-up celebration than pin-the-tail-on-the-donkey at home with birthday cake. And grown-up suits me, for today I am eleven years old. I was born on October 4th, 1907, in this very house with its yellow clapboards and black shutters — both in need of paint, I'm afraid — and with its big porch and the forsythia bushes across the front of the yard. I was born upstairs in this house eleven years ago in Portland, Maine.

But now I am desolate. The Portland Board of Health has issued an order suddenly that no gatherings are to be held at theaters or motion picture houses or dance halls. None at all! And schools are to be closed as well. All because of a sickness that has arrived in Maine. It is called Spanish influenza. I do not know a single person who suffers from it and think it is all quite silly and it has completely ruined my birthday.

But for the occasion Mother and Father have given me this lovely journal to record my thoughts. I am only sorry that my thoughts are so distressed.

Later

Oh! I am adding this later! Mother has given me a special gift. She said she had been saving it for when I was older, perhaps thirteen, but she was sorry my birthday celebration has been canceled, and so she thought to give me this now. It is a ring, a beautiful gold ring, with an opal stone, and it was my grandmother's. I never knew my grandmother, for all my grandparents died before I was born. But her hands must have been small. The ring fits me exactly, and I will wear it forever.

Saturday, October 5, 1918

Driving automobiles on Sunday has been outlawed for some time so as to conserve fuel for the war effort. But today it was announced that automobiles may be used tomorrow, so that people might have a day in the countryside and away from the crowded parts of the city where infection is spreading.

I would like a day in the country! But we do not have an automobile. Few people do. They are very costly, sometimes as much as $600. Father is only a store clerk, though he hopes to be manager of the store before too long. He works very hard and says that he will see to it that all of his children, even the girls, go to college. But we are not rich.

In the spring, before Lucy was born, we sometimes took the electric trolley up to the town of Gray. Uncle Henry would meet us there and drive us in his horse and wagon to the farm. Mother likes to see her brother, Uncle Henry, even though his wife, my aunt Sarah, is somewhat ill-tempered. Uncle Henry and Aunt Sarah have six children! There are three older boys who help a lot with the farm: John, Joseph, and Robert. Then twin girls named Margaret and Mabel, who are ten and very lively. And a small boy, little more than a baby, named Willie. No wonder Aunt Sarah is so ill-tempered, with all those children to care for! It is quite an adventure to go there.

They live in the countryside, just what Maine Fuel Administrator Hamlen says we need! But we do not own an automobile, and Mother says it is too hard to make the trip on the trolley with the baby so small. We must wait until Lucy is six months old, Mother says, and it will be easier. That is three more months! I am hoping, though, that we might go to Uncle Henry's farm at Christmas.

And I am wishing that someone with an automobile would invite us for a ride tomorrow.

Beds have been put into the Italian church on Fore Street, so that people living in crowded houses where relatives are sick can go there to sleep and get away from the influenza.

I would certainly not want to sleep in a church with a lot of strangers. I like my own room with its flowered wallpaper and ruffled curtains. My dollhouse sits on the floor beside the window, with the little people inside lying stiffly on their beds, and the tiny roast chicken on the kitchen table as it has been for years. My bed has a spread on it embroidered with sunflowers. My books are lined up on a shelf in the corner, and the lamp on the table beside my bed has a shepherdess on the shade, her painted hand forever above her forehead, as she forever looks across the pale green meadow for her sheep.

Lucy still sleeps in her little crib in my parents' bedroom, beside their big bed, so that Mother can tend her when she wakes at night. When she is older she will share my room. I hope she never becomes the kind of child who grabs and breaks things! I will teach her to be careful.

At night, when everything is quiet, I can hear the tall clock ticking at the foot of the stairs. Father winds it each evening, checking the time against his pocket watch, sometimes moving one of the metal hands a tiny bit. Each hour it chimes, and from my bed I always hear the nine chimes and tell myself that I will stay awake to hear ten. But I never have.

Sunday, October 6, 1918

Even our church on Woodford Street has closed now, and so we could not go to Sunday School today. It is a little frightening and odd, big solid places like churches closing. The Catholic churches are holding their services out of doors. But our church has simply closed and so we held our own little service at home, and said the Lord's Prayer at breakfast. Then Father read a psalm. Daniel was disrespectful and had to be punished. Mother told me later that fourteen is a very difficult age for a boy and she wishes Father would not be quite so harsh.

I wanted to walk to Emily Ann Walsh's house on Rackleff Street and play there this afternoon. Emily Ann and I have been reading *The Secret Garden* together and acting it out. We take turns being Mary. It is especially fun in the beginning, when she is so sulky and tries to order the servants about! Now we have just reached the part where she finds the garden. We were planning to act that part in the Walshes' backyard, where they have some thick lilacs, but Mother telephoned and found that Mrs. Walsh has taken ill. Mother thinks it is not the influenza but just a fall cold. Still, they should not have company because even a cold is contagious and she does not want me to catch it and give it to Lucy, who is still so small.

The newspaper says that fresh air is the best way to combat the flu. So I think that playing in Emily Ann's backyard would have been a very healthy thing to do. I did not say that to Mother because it would have been arguing, and she has already had to talk to Daniel this morning about his disrespectful attitude.

Because we couldn't go anyplace, I actually did some schoolwork this afternoon. Daniel has been helping me with South America. He is fond of maps and knows a great deal about the world. But I can never keep the South American countries straight in my mind (Chile is easy because it is so long and thin. And Brazil, so large! But the rest! Well, each one seems the same as the others!) and my teacher said I must work on learning them before the next test.

Daniel actually drew me a map with just the outlines of the countries. Then I had to fill in the names. I mixed up Uruguay and Paraguay once again! He devised a trick to help me remember: I think of the word *up* lying on its side, and if you look, you will see the P — Paraguay — up above the U. It seems to work. Daniel is very clever. I still have trouble with Bolivia, though.

He said he would quiz me again tomorrow, so I must study my map. In return I told him I will help him with his French. Not that I know French! But I will read the list of vocabulary words to him and check to be sure he spells them correctly. He finds French very tedious.

Mother is worrying about tomorrow because Marie, the laundress, has sent word that she cannot come. Marie lives near Fore Street, in the Italian section of Portland, and there is much sickness there. But what is Mother to do, with Lucy's diapers, and the sheets, as well, to be washed? I suppose I will have to help.

I wish there would be school tomorrow. Then Daniel and I would not be confined in this house together, where — except when we are doing our schoolwork — he is determined to thwart and torture me in every way. He hid the book I was reading, *Hans Brinker*, just when I was at a very exciting part. Then he made me guess where it was by asking twenty yes-or-no questions: "Is it in the living room?" "No." "Is it in the kitchen?" "No." "Is it in the dining room?" "Yes." Well, that narrowed it down, but the dining room has a large buffet, with drawers — each drawer a separate question — and also a closet, and just when I was running out of ideas, because all my questions got "no" answers, I thought to ask, "Is it behind a curtain?" which was a "Yes!" But there are long, thick curtains at every window in the dining room, and he said I must ask them one by one — but I only had three questions left by then! I made a lucky guess and found my book, but he had lost my bookmark and I had a hard time finding my place.

Mother sighed and said, "Daniel, don't torment your sister so!" but he paid no attention. And in truth I saw Mother laughing a bit as I searched and searched for my book. So I am not entirely sure she was on my side.

(I plan to hide Daniel's shoes when I have an opportunity. One will go into the umbrella stand just inside the front door. The other, I think, into the box where the milkman collects our empty bottles and leaves full ones. Daniel will never find them! Maybe I will charge him a penny for each, when I reveal where they are.)

As for Father, he ignored our fuss, as he always does, and went into the living room and read the newspaper. These days more news is about the influenza than about the war. He says they are making too much of it. He intends to go to work tomorrow and every day to follow, and he expects his fellow employees at the store to do the same. He thinks Mayor Clarke is a fool to close down a whole city.

Monday, October 7, 1918

So soon after I had made a vow never to remove my grandmother's ring, I removed it in order to help Mother this morning with the laundry. I placed it carefully on the kitchen windowsill, where it sparkled in the light. But, oh, after we began boiling all the water for washing Lucy's diapers and bed things, the windows became so steamed that we could not even see outdoors!

Fortunately the weather is fine, with sunshine, and we were able to hang the wet laundry out on the line, where it dried quickly in the breeze. I put myself in charge of that: hanging everything in neat rows, then bringing it in as it dried, and folding, folding, folding.

Daniel agreed, though in an ill temper, to lift the heavy tubs of water to empty them. Mother cannot do it alone. Nor can Marie, though she is very strong. Mother always helps her with the lifting.

Lucy was very agreeable this morning. We put her in her carriage on the back porch, for fresh air, and she kicked her legs under the blanket, and smiled. She was watching the breeze move the tree leaves, I think (some leaves are falling now, and they blow around). I could see her blue eyes moving back and forth, following. Then after a bit she fell asleep.

Father walked home from the store at lunchtime, as he always does, and praised us for doing Marie's work so well. Then he noticed that we had not found time to prepare a meal! But he was good-natured, and we stopped our labors for a bit and sliced yesterday's roast and buttered some bread.

Daniel came in hungry, too. He had gone up the street to the Farlows' house on Seeley Avenue and had been helping Martin Farlow repair a bicycle. Martin was supposed to be back at college by now, but Colby has postponed its opening because of the flu. Even that far away, in Waterville, people are ill!

Mother took a moment at lunchtime to telephone the Walshes' house and found that Emily Ann's mother is feeling a little better. But their next-door neighbor, Mrs. Flynn, newly married and expecting, is very, very ill, and the doctor has not yet found time to come. All the doctors are busy and the hospitals are filling up. Mrs. Flynn's husband stayed home from his office and is trying to take care of her, but there is really not much to be done, Mrs. Walsh says, just to wipe her face with cool cloths and to urge her to have some broth. Her fever is very high and from time to time her nose bleeds. She does not recognize her husband, which pains him terribly.

Father says a few customers are still coming to the store, but the city streets are quite deserted, and many of those who are out and about are wearing gauze masks. I do not like to picture that in my mind: people with masks. It scares me. Mother said perhaps he should not return to work, but he was shocked at the idea. "What if everyone left their jobs?" he asked. "The city would cease to be!"

In truth I think he did not want to stay at home while all the laundry was being done, with the windows so steamed and the harsh smell of soap everywhere.

"Where's the baby?" Father asked, and when Mother told him, he went to the back porch and kissed Lucy, who was still sleeping soundly with her tiny fingers curled into her hands. Then he took an apple from the bowl on the kitchen table, folded the newspaper, and walked off again, down to Stevens Avenue and around the corner.

When the laundry was finally finished, I put my ring back on and secretly hoped that Marie would be back soon, school would reopen, and I would not have to do laundry again, maybe ever in my life.

Tuesday, October 8, 1918

Young Mrs. Flynn died during the night. We heard this from Emily Ann's mother, who was weeping when she called. She said Mrs. Flynn just got worse and worse, and didn't recognize anyone, and toward the end could not breathe, and there was nothing they could do. Now her poor husband is very ill and there is no one to tend him. No doctors will come.

Volunteers, most of them women, are moving about the city by automobile, carrying soup and bread into homes where people are afflicted. But there is not much else they can do.

Father came home early and does not want supper. He feels very, very tired.

Wednesday, October 16, 1918

I have not written for eight days.

What could I write?

Father is dead.

Mother is dead.

My baby sister, Lucy, is dead.

Daniel and I are alive, but Daniel hates the entire world and will not speak, not to me or to anyone.

He and I are at Uncle Henry's farm now. It is a cold and crowded place. I overhear Uncle Henry and Aunt Sarah talking in low voices filled with both sorrow and anger.

I do not know what will become of me and Daniel.

I can remember the last words my mother said to me, but I cannot bring myself to write them down.

I had my birthday just twelve days ago. I am eleven years old. I feel one hundred.

Friday, October 18, 1918

In Rockland they have turned a large hotel, the Narragansett, into an emergency hospital, and anyone of any class or religion may go there, without reference to their financial circumstances. Women from eight different churches have become an emergency hospital committee, and the Superintendent of Schools has announced that the city's school teachers will now become workers in the hospital office, kitchen, and sterilizing department. The world has turned upside down. Nothing will ever be the same.

The *Courier Gazette* has printed a list of needs: towels, sheets, blankets, and babies' cribs. Reading it made me remember Lucy's little crib at home, and I wept. I wondered what would become of our house. I suppose when all of this ends (surely it will end!) some other family will move in and pay the rent. What of our things? We did not have valuable things but there were things we loved. Mother's good dishes, with pink flowers painted around the edge. The tall clock, and the umbrella stand where once I thought I would hide Daniel's shoe. What of them?

We left so quickly and took so little. It is a blur in my memory. Uncle Henry made whatever arrangements had to be made. But he was silent, and rushed. I could tell he wanted to get away. It had become a house of horror. He hurried us, and I left with only the clothes I wore and a small satchel with a yellow scarf that Mother had knitted for me and my Sunday School shoes (why did I take those, I wonder? But I was not thinking clearly) and my beloved book, *The Secret Garden.*

It happened to Mary Lennox, too. In the book, I mean. She became an orphan and was taken from her home and sent to live with an uncle. When Emily Ann and I were reading it together and acting it out, it seemed like make-believe, and we were very dramatic, each of us weeping wildly when it was our turn to be Mary, while the other held the book and tried to look serious. But we giggled, both of us.

Mary's uncle, Archibald Craven, in the book, seems very uncaring. Reading it, I thought he was cruel. Now, though, watching Uncle Henry, whose face is stern and lined, who seems uncaring, I realize something. He is grieving. He loved my mother. She was his only sister. But men cannot weep. They must do things. They must make arrangements, take care of things, make plans, figure things out. Uncle Henry must mourn his sister and at the same time figure out where to put two more children, and how to feed them (for there is little money), and he must also answer to his very angry wife, who doesn't want us here (I have heard her say just that).

And he must find a way to deal with Daniel, who either falls sullenly silent, or talks back rudely when asked to help with chores. I don't blame Daniel, really, because I have seen how the boys — our cousins — mock him for not knowing how to do things on a farm. But I fear Uncle Henry will have to thrash him. Father would have, I know. With his belt.

I try to help but am always in the way. Aunt Sarah says that she is forever tripping over me. The twins, Margaret and Mabel, tried at first to be sweet and loving, but now they are cross because I am sleeping in their room and taking the space where they always played with their dolls. And I am wearing their clothes, as well! They don't like that. But what am I to do?

I wander, often. I button up my jacket and walk down the lane and through the meadow. The air is getting cold now. The wildflowers have all died back and the grass snaps under my feet. Uncle Henry's workhorses come to the fence hoping I have brought them a treat, and sometimes I find forgotten apples on the ground that I can feed to them. One morning there was a thin layer of ice on their water trough. I poked it with a stick and broke through easily. But soon the water will be frozen solid. Winters are hard here. Uncle Henry and his boys (and Daniel, if he ever returns to himself) will have to carve a path through snow to the barn and carry water and feed for the animals.

Schools are still closed everywhere. The sickness does not seem to end. It is terribly frightening. At Swans Island, they say, out of a population of 800, there are 260 who are desperately ill.

The sky is almost always gray. I wonder if my mother looks down on me.

I will tell you now, the last thing she said. For a while it was too hard for me to remember it or say it. But now I think of her so often, and of that last day. Father had come home from work tired, and didn't want supper, and then very suddenly he became terribly ill. Mother tended him and would not let us near. She was trying to keep us safe. Daniel and I tried to help a bit. I cooked what food I knew how to, and Daniel tended the fires in the woodstoves.

Then the baby, too, was ill, all of a sudden. The doctor did come, once, but he just shook his head and went away again. He seemed so tired. And so did Mother. But she told me what to do: to bring the food to the door of the bedroom, to leave it there on the floor and go away. I brought basins of water, too, and cloths, and left them there for her, but she always told me to move away, not to come near to her. So I would leave the tray, knock on the door, then stand at the top of the stairs and talk to her from there, when she opened it a crack to take the things.

Lucy never cried, not once. It would have made my heart leap to hear Lucy cry, but she was silent in her sickness.

I could see when Mother fell ill. She still came to the door of the room where they were and spoke to me, but she was weakened and feverish.

It was more than just tired. Sometimes her mind wandered.

I knew the doctor would not return, but Daniel told me to run next door and ask Mrs. O'Brien to come and help us. She has always been such a kind and caring neighbor. But she came to the door twisting her hands in her apron, and said no. She said she was sorry but there was nothing she could do.

I telephoned Mrs. Walsh, Emily Ann's mother. She said the same thing but that she would pray for us.

I went and stood on the front porch, looking down toward Stevens Avenue with a feeling of hopelessness. Ordinarily there would be people walking, horses and buggies, occasionally an automobile. But now it was empty. If I had called out, "Help us!" there would have been no one to hear it. The houses in the neighborhood were all silent, with shades drawn. A dog came past slowly, looking back and forth, as if it had become lost.

Finally, not knowing what else to do, I went into the kitchen and made more tea. I put it into the Blue Willow teapot, and then put that on a tray with a clean cup and saucer. I balanced it carefully, walking as if I were serving a lovely luncheon, and took it upstairs. Carefully I set it down outside the door to Mother and Father's room, and knocked, as I had been doing. Then I stood back.

Mother came after a long moment. She smiled a little at me.

"You're a lamb," she said. "You're my dear little lamb."

She looked down at the teapot, sighed a bit, and then closed the door, leaving the tray as it was.

After that I did not see her again, and there came no reply to my knocks. We waited awhile. Then Daniel said we must try again to find help. He telephoned Uncle Henry, who said he would come as quickly as possible. Daniel and I sat silently in the living room for hours, waiting. The tall clock was no longer ticking. Father was the one who had wound it every evening, and now its metal hands were still. It was evening when at last we heard Uncle Henry's steps on the front porch. He came in and Daniel and I followed him up the stairs.

But by then it was too late. When he opened the door to the room, I cried out at what I saw. Daniel's face turned white. He came and put his arms around me. He held tight to me, but it felt as if the hallway where we stood was spinning and whirling. I remember nothing after that.

Saturday, October 19, 1918

Walking in the lane beside the farm this morning, I found five stones that I have put into my pocket. The two larger ones are the mother and the father. *My* mother and father: Caroline and Walter Pierce. Then there is a slightly smaller one, grayish, with a jagged stripe and a rough edge: That is Daniel. A sweet, tiny pinkish one is Lucy. And I am an ordinary stone. There is nothing special about me, Lydia Amelia Pierce, except that I am a part of this little family in my pocket.

I stayed outdoors too long and Aunt Sarah was very angry when I went back. I had promised to help with the bread making, but I forgot. Margaret and Mabel helped but that left no one to look after Willie, who is two, and he got into Aunt Sarah's knitting and pulled it all apart. So she was in a rage.

And Daniel left his chores undone as well.

Later I heard Aunt Sarah say to Uncle Henry that "they" must go. By "they" she means me and Daniel. I could hear Uncle Henry sigh but he did not argue with her. Listening, I touched my fingers to the stones in my pocket and hummed loudly so that I could put her angry voice out of my thoughts.

But I heard her tell him to take us to Sabbathday Lake, and so I think she means for him to drown us. Surely he would not do that to his dead sister's children! But I did not hear him say no to his wife's command.

Sunday, October 20, 1918

Daniel told me he hopes the war in Europe will last and last so that when he is old enough he can go and join up. He is only fourteen. In February he will be fifteen. But that is still not old enough for the army, and anyway people say now that the war will end soon.

There is little talk of it anymore. A year ago, when Mr. and Mrs. Andrews, of Portland, lost their son, Harold, in a battle in France, Mother took a bouquet of flowers to their home. He was the first soldier from Maine to die in the war, and everyone spoke of it in shocked and saddened voices. Then there were so many others.

But when the influenza began, we forgot the war because the horrors moved into our own homes. And now Daniel says he would like to join up. Anything, he says, to get away from Uncle Henry's farm.

He does not talk to me much but I found him out behind the barn, whittling on a piece of wood, when I took a walk to escape the twins bickering and Willie howling and Aunt Sarah complaining. Uncle Henry and the older boys were out repairing the fences, and Daniel should have gone to help, but instead he was crouched behind the barn. I asked him if he knew where Sabbathday

Lake was and he shrugged and said no.

"I think Uncle Henry is fixing to drown us, the way he does kittens," I said.

Daniel just laughed a bit and carved at his stick. "He doesn't have to drown *me*," he said. "If he wants me gone, I'll go, and glad to."

"But where?" I asked, for I had been thinking the same way myself. I have no wish to stay at a farm where I am not wanted.

That's when Daniel said about the war, and the army. He could lie about his age, he said. Others have. Maybe in the spring he would try.

"I have to wait till spring because I've got no winter shoes, not good enough for walking far." He held up one foot and I could see that his shoes were in poor shape, with one sole loose and aflap. Poor Daniel. That he would think war might be better than the life he had! It made me sad—and a little angry, too, that he would leave me behind without a second thought. But he was not really the Daniel I had known. When I looked closely at him, I could see he looked untended, his clothes filthy, his hair needing a cut. I suppose I am much the same, in my borrowed dress and torn stockings stuck with twigs and burrs. We have been only ten days here at the farm and already we look like the orphans that we are, disheveled and dirty.

Monday, October 21, 1918

Tonight at supper Uncle Henry told Daniel and me to get our things together because he would be taking us someplace in the morning. He did not say where. But I think if he were planning to drown us like kittens, he would not tell us to bring clean underclothes.

United Society of Shakers

Sabbathday Lake, Maine

Tuesday, October 22, 1918

So much has happened and I hardly know where to begin.

We left in the middle of the morning, this morning, after the farm chores were done. We were dirty yet. Daniel didn't care. But I felt ashamed. No matter where we were going — and I still didn't know — I did not want to arrive smelly and smudged. But Aunt Sarah would not let me have a bath. I washed my face and hands at the sink, as I have each day. But truly, I was not clean, not at all.

The well is always low by fall, especially after a dry summer, so I understood her reason. If I had a bath, it might mean a long wait until there was water again, enough to wash the dishes and the clothes. And so I simply scrubbed what I could and cleaned my nails. I put on the dress I had worn from Portland when we left there, for I could not take the twins' clothes and wouldn't have wanted to.

It was eight miles to the northwest. A beautiful day, cool, with a breeze, and the trees all red and gold as they are in October, with many leaves on the ground already. The horses are eager in cool weather; they snort and stamp. We had brought some food and had our lunch along the way, stopping by a stream where the horses could have a drink. It was only when we stopped that Uncle Henry began to talk, suddenly.

"You know I'm taking you to the Shakers," he said.

But Daniel and I just looked at each other. Of course we didn't know that. We didn't even know what it meant. Shakers?

"The Shakers at Sabbathday Lake." Uncle Henry carved his apple with his knife. He ate a piece, and wiped his beard with the napkin Aunt Sarah had placed in the basket with the food. He looked off into the distance, across the hills and woodland that bordered the road. "Your mother and I learned to swim at that lake when we were your age," he said.

"Were the Shakers there then?" I asked him. I pictured Uncle Henry as a boy Daniel's size, and my mother, his sister, Caroline, younger. In my mind I could see them playing on the shore of a lake, and surrounding them was a group of something mysterious, shaking. I decided Uncle Henry was telling us a ghost story, as he sometimes did. "Were you scared?" I asked.

He reached over and smoothed my hair. "You look like your mother," he said, and I could see that he felt both sad and kindly at once.

"I know," I told him.

Daniel became impatient. He scribbled with a stick in the dirt. "What are the Shakers?" he asked gruffly.

Uncle Henry sighed. "Their village is up ahead. We'll be there soon. They're expecting us."

"And you're leaving us there." I said it in a way that wasn't a question, because I knew it was true.

"I'll try to come back to see you. But you understand that we can't keep you with us."

I nodded. I understood. It was simply that Uncle Henry and Aunt Sarah didn't have enough. Not enough room. Not enough money. Not enough food. As for Daniel, he just looked away.

Uncle Henry began gathering the scraps from lunch. He tossed his apple core into the bushes. "The Shakers take in children and raise them. They're fair and hardworking and honest. You'll get good care, and an education. You'll get what I can't give you."

He held out his hand to help me back up into the wagon. Daniel hoisted himself up on the other side. Uncle Henry took a handkerchief from his pocket and wiped his face as if he were sweating, the way he did during farm work. But I could see he had tears in his eyes. He settled himself in his seat and jiggled the reins so that the horses started up.

"They'll seem strange to you at first. They have some strange customs. It's their religion."

"My friend Marjorie Fallon, in Portland? She's Catholic. Catholic is a strange religion."

Uncle Henry laughed a bit. He reached over and drew me to him, put his arm around me, for the first time since he came for us in Portland. He was so stern then, so silent. Now there was a softer part to him showing, and I knew he loved us and was sorry to send us away.

"I should have said *different*, not strange," he explained. "But you'll grow used to their ways. I had a hired man once, Levi Mitchell. Raised by the Shakers. He didn't stay there, once he was grown. Left there to make his own way, and worked for me for a while. Best worker I ever had. Careful, and quiet. Always bowed his head for a minute before he ate. He could read and write and figure, and he knew farm work. He said the Shakers taught him all of it, and he had nothing but good to say of them.

"I was thinking of Levi when I telephoned them to ask if they could take you."

"But he didn't stay," Daniel said suddenly. It was the first he'd spoken in a while.

"No, he decided he wanted to be in the world. That's what the Shakers call our way of life."

"I don't want to stay," Daniel said.

Uncle Henry looked at him. "You need a place, son. You need a home. They'll give you that for now. When the time comes, you can decide."

Daniel looked away, and I could tell that he had already decided. No one said anything. The horses plodded along, and when we rounded a curve in the road, we could see, first, a huge brick building, then the others, all of them white, that were near it. We could see cattle in the fields behind the barn — and glimpses of the lake beyond. An orchard spread out on our left, and beyond it what looked like a schoolhouse. It seemed to be a whole village, but quite small, and it was amazingly tidy. It made me think of a toy village, built for dolls.

"Here we are," Uncle Henry said.

Now I am sitting in the room where I am to live. A woman brought me here. Other girls will share this room with me, but they are not here now. Their beds are neatly made, and everything is so clean, so in order. At home in Portland, our house was clean, but nothing like this. I sit here for a moment trying to understand the difference and I realize there is no decoration here. At home, there were pretty scarves on the bureaus, pictures on the walls, framed photographs, a vase of flowers, a stack of magazines, a bowl of mints. There was my lamp with the shepherdess looking into the pale green meadow.

At Uncle Henry's, nothing was very pretty, and everything was atumble, always. Toys scattered, and things half-finished: a partly knitted sweater; stockings waiting to be darned; wood stacked haphazardly, toppled, and then left.

Here everything is bare. The wood is polished, the floor and windows spotless, and in its own way, this room is beautiful. But there is no decoration. Drawers are built into the wall, and I have been shown which is mine. Pegs on the wall are to hold hanging things. There are two chairs, wooden ones with woven seats.

There is nothing else.

Sister Jennie (I will tell you more about her when I have time) is kind enough, though I can tell I must not try her patience. And she is to come for me in a moment, to tell me what to do next, so I will put my journal now into the drawer that is mine. And the stones from my pocket: my little family. I will put them here, under the pillow on my bed.

So already I have secrets.

Later

I have cried, now, until there are no tears left in me.

Where to begin? I will start where I left off earlier today. There was no time to write more then, for I was taken from this place to that, and not much alone. I need to be alone to write. Now I am, for I am being punished.

It is odd to think of being alone as punishment, for I love time to myself. Mother always punished me, when I needed it (and I often did, I confess), with extra chores. Father, with his belt, though he was never cruel, not really.

Here they do not punish with a thrashing, not even the boys, I am told, but with separation. So I am here alone in my retiring room (that is what they call the bedroom. They seem to have a different language) until the other girls come up to bed, and I do not mind at all, though I have cried very loudly, just to make them all sorry, hearing me.

So now I will go back to earlier, when we arrived. A boy came and took the reins and led the horses away, I suppose to give them water. Uncle Henry took us into a building where we sat in a hallway to wait. It was very quiet and dimly lit, and cool. Uncle Henry went into a room where there was a woman in an odd dress, and Daniel and I could not hear what he and she were saying, though we tried to.

After a while a man came into the hallway. He nodded to Daniel, completely ignoring me, which I thought was rude, and asked Daniel to come with him. I expected Daniel to argue and refuse. But to my surprise, he simply picked up his small bag of things and went away with the man, without a word to me. Of course I didn't think he would say good-bye! We are both here in this same small place, of course, and would likely see each other shortly. But still! He should have made some acknowledgment of me, I thought, and certainly he should have introduced me to the man. I decided I would mention it to Daniel when I saw him next because even if we have to stay here for a while, we must not forget the manners that our mother worked so hard to teach us.

So now I was alone in the hallway, and peeking into the room where Uncle Henry was, I could see that he was reading some papers and had a pen in his hand, as if he were to sign them. But that was all I saw, because suddenly a woman appeared and came to where I was. I could not tell how old she was. She wore glasses, had her hair pulled back tight and wore a small cap over it, and her long-sleeved dress was to her ankles and of a dark pattern. The front of her dress had a piece of the same fabric that fell across her bosom, like a sort of bib, and shaped in a triangle. I have never seen a dress like it before.

She told me she was Sister Jennie Mathers. So I realized she was a kind of nun, for I remembered my friend Marjorie Fallon in Portland. Marjorie attends St. Joseph's, and she used to speak of her favorite teacher, Sister Agatha, and her *least* favorite, Sister Mary Eunice. The dress that Sister Jennie wore was not at all like what the nuns at St. Joseph's wore, but this is a different place and the rules and uniforms are likely different. I decided that if they told me to make promises that would turn me into a Catholic, or worse — into a nun! — I would do so with my fingers crossed, which makes everything invalid.

Sister Jennie knew my name, and said it in a warm and kindly way. "Welcome to Chosen Land, Lydia," she said.

I must have looked puzzled, because she explained, "It's our spiritual name. Each community has one. Over in Canterbury, they call their community Holy Ground."

"Oh, I see," I said, though I didn't, really. Chosen Land? Holy Ground? Everything seemed very confusing.

"You come along with me," she said. "I'll take you to the girls' shop."

I am sorry to say that I rose and followed her, carrying my small satchel, and forgot to speak to Uncle Henry. I suppose I thought I would be seeing him again, but that was not to be true. The last I saw of my mother's brother was the back of him, sitting in a straight wooden chair, leaning over the papers on the desk and signing me away to the Shakers.

"What will I be selling?" I asked Sister Jennie.
She looked puzzled. "Selling?"

"You said we were going to the shop."

She laughed. "It's just our way of naming things. It's where you'll live, with the other girls. We call it the girls' shop. Over here —" She pointed to a building on her right. "That's the boys' shop. Your brother will be living there."

"It's very pretty here," I said politely to Sister Jennie as we walked on the path between the buildings. And I did not have to cross my fingers when I said it, for it was indeed quite beautiful, all the buildings so clean and white, and the pastures beyond still green in October, with the trees every shade of orange and red.

"It's lovely in summer, with the flower gardens," Sister Jennie said. "Of course it's too late now for flowers. But next summer, you'll see. Some of our girls make the most beautiful bouquets and we sell them up at the Mansion House."

I was completely befuddled by what she said. A mansion house, like the one in *The Secret Garden*? I didn't see anything of the sort. I saw only the white house she was leading me to, and it was not at all a mansion, though it was large, larger than my home in Portland. It had porches, and looked comfortable enough.

"Where are the girls?" I asked her, for it seemed so quiet everywhere. "In school?"

"Nay," she said. "The schoolhouse is closed for now, because of the sickness."

It was the first time — though not the last! — that I heard Sister Jennie say "Nay" instead of "No." It seemed very old-fashioned and odd.

"The girls are working all about," she said. "Susannah's in the kitchen of the dwelling, helping with the after-dinner work there. She's just your age, eleven. And Rebecca's at the ironing. She's ten."

She had gestured a bit, with her head, to indicate the big brick building when she described Susannah at work in the kitchen. And the ironing, it seemed, was in the large white building behind the one we were now entering.

"And I left the other girls doing fancywork," she said. "They're in here."

We went in through the back door, the one off the rear porch. I could see a room full of stacked wood facing me, ready for winter. And next, a bathroom! I was so glad to see it, and that they did not have a privy like Uncle Henry's. Awful, smelly thing! But this was clean and bright, with a tub standing on feet.

She saw me looking at it, smiled, and indicated with a nod of her head that I might use it. And thank goodness, for I think I might have burst otherwise, but had not wanted to ask.

When I came out, she was waiting, and she said to me, "Tonight you will have a warm bath." I know she meant, "because you are so dirty," but she was kind not to say it. And in truth I loved the thought of a bath, the smell of soap, the softness of a towel. There was none of that at Uncle Henry's.

She led me into a large front room where a small group of young girls sat on the wooden chairs that I had seen everywhere. They were quite silent but looked at me curiously, and one, a little younger than I, with curls and freckles, gave me a grin. Sister Jennie introduced them and they were not called "Sister," so I know they were not yet nuns. I have forgotten, already, most of the names, but the one who had grinned at me was Grace. Each of them was at work with her hands, most knitting, some working on samplers with cross-stitch. I surely hoped that they had time to play, and to run about outdoors. *If I have to sit silently in this room and knit*, I thought, *I will faint from boredom.*

I noticed a book on a table, and Sister Jennie saw me notice. "I was reading aloud to the girls while they did their handwork," she explained.

"*The Five Little Peppers*," the girl named Grace piped up. "It's a lovely story."

I knew, for I had read it myself already at home. "I brought a book with me," I said. "It's called *The Secret Garden*." I reached down and took it out of my satchel, to show them.

To my surprise, Sister Jennie took it out of my hands. "We'll place it here, on the shelf, with the other books," she said.

"But it's mine," I told her.

"Nay," she said. "All that we have belongs to us all."

So I watched as my beloved book, the one I had hoped to have in my room — wherever my room was to be — so that I could read in private, became part of their small collection of books.

And for that reason, I was downhearted when she led me up the stairs. The girls turned back to their handwork, and I followed Sister Jennie to the large room above. There were four beds, and she told me I was to have the one that had been Eliza's. I wondered what had become of Eliza but didn't ask.

She showed me the drawer in which to place my things, and left me there to settle myself. It was then, seated there on Eliza's bed, which was now mine, that I wrote earlier in this journal.

Shortly after I finished and put the journal into a drawer, a bell rang. I think it was on the top of the large brick building nearby. Sister Jennie summoned me and I went with her and the other girls, after washing our hands, to that building, for supper. By then I was certainly hungry!

But we waited for quite a while outside of the dining room, sitting there quietly in a room that seemed almost like the doctor's waiting room in Portland. Older girls came in, and then the women, who were dressed as Sister Jennie was, wearing the long-sleeved dress with its V-shaped yoke, and a cap covering their tightly pulled-back hair. Some of them greeted me in soft voices, and I learned their names: Sister Helen, Sister Amanda, Eldress Prudence, Eldress Lizzie.

I wondered where the men were, and the boys. I wanted to see Daniel. But when I asked, whispering, Sister Jennie told me that they entered through a different door. She called them "the brethren."

I was a little nervous because I was afraid there would be rules I didn't know to follow. I was going to ask Sister Jennie. But suddenly there was a chime, and the door to the dining room opened. I watched and could see that we would enter in a particular way, with Eldress Lizzie first, then Eldress Prudence. Behind them, in twos, the other women. Then the teen-aged girls, and finally we youngest girls, and Sister Jennie with us. She directed me to a table in what seemed to be the children's section. I was to sit with three other girls, the three who would share the bedroom with me—curly-headed Grace; Polly, who wears glasses; and Rebecca, who seems so quiet and serious.

After we had entered and were standing at our places, another door opened and the men came in, followed by boys. There was Daniel! He didn't see me at first. And I couldn't help it—I called his name and left my place to scurry across to the other side of the room where they were finding their tables. I just wanted to let him know that I was all right, that I was here. I was going to greet him and then hurry back to my seat. Supper hadn't started. It didn't occur to me that I was doing anything wrong.

But Sister Jennie grabbed me. She almost ran across the room to grab my arm and move me back firmly to where I had been. I was so confused. "That's my brother," I began to explain. "I was only going to . . ."

Then I realized that the entire room was silent,

and that everyone was looking at me. I stopped talking. The women and a girl my age who had been working in the kitchen appeared in the door. By now I was back at my chair. And then everyone got on their knees, on the floor, and bowed their heads. I did the same. They were praying silently. I couldn't pray. I could feel tears starting, hot behind my eyelids, and I bit my tongue to keep from crying. Finally, after a moment, we all stood, pulled out our chairs, and sat down. Food was brought to each table by the women from the kitchen, and by the young girl, Susannah, who lives in the girls' shop. She smiled at me curiously and I guessed they had told her that a new girl had arrived.

I don't remember what the food was. There was plenty of it, and I ate. But I was tired and confused and embarrassed and scared. The whole meal was silent. No one talked. I glanced across the room from time to time at Daniel, but he didn't look up.

I do remember there was apple pie, and that I had two pieces.

Then the meal was over. I watched the other

girls and placed my knife and fork carefully, exactly the way they had placed theirs. Eldress Lizzie stood and nodded, and it seemed to mean that we should all march out in order. Grace grinned at me a little impishly, and she walked beside me back along the path to the girls' shop. Talking seemed to be allowed now, and Grace asked, "Where did you live, in the world?"

I almost laughed, it was such an odd way of asking. Was this not still the world? "Portland," I told her.

"I lived in Harrison," she said. "I came here last March. My mother died."

"I'm sorry," I whispered. And I was, for I knew what it was like. "Do you have any brothers? Or sisters?"

"All of us are sisters," Grace explained, as if it didn't seem strange to her as she said it, though it surely did to me. "And brethren, too, but we stay separate. That's why Sister Jennie pulled you back from the brethren's side."

"But I just wanted to speak to Daniel! He's my *real* brother!"

We were approaching the porch and the entrance to the girls' shop. Sister Jennie appeared at my side. She had overheard what I had said to Grace. "We are all real brethren and sisters here," she said in a gentle voice, "but we'll arrange a meeting with Daniel for you soon."

"A *meeting*?" I asked. It sounded so formal and odd.

"We don't converse with the brethren, or get near. It's part of Mother Ann's teachings. You will grow accustomed to it and see the wisdom in it.

"Girls!" Sister Jennie called to the others, who were standing and talking quietly on the porch. "We'll gather in the front room. Polly? Would you lead the others in some singing? I'll take our new girl and help her with a bath."

I almost told her no. I don't need to be helped to take a bath! I am eleven years old! But I was just so tired. Everything here is so different and puzzling. And so I followed her into the first-floor bathroom and waited as she turned on the water in the deep tub. While it ran (and I touched it with my finger. It was so warm and soothing), Sister Jennie disappeared briefly and returned with a folded garment.

"I think this nightdress will fit you," she said.

"I have no other clothes with me," I explained, as I began to take off the dusty dress I had worn all day, the same one I had worn when I left my life in Portland behind. I was embarrassed. "I had so many dresses, but things happened so quickly and somehow they were all left behind, and I don't know . . ."

"It doesn't matter, child. You will be provided for. I sew clothes for all my girls. Tomorrow we will give you underclothes, and there are dresses of all sizes in the large closet."

She handed me a thick bar of soap and waited while I stepped into the filled tub. It did feel grand to lower myself into the warm water after such a long time without. "Wash your hair, too, and I'll come back to help with combing it when you're ready," Sister Jennie said.

I nodded. I could hear the girls singing in the front room. The melodies were unfamiliar. She left me, taking my little heap of dirty clothing with her, and I lay soaking in the tub and listened to the girls' voices after I was alone. Then I scrubbed myself until my flesh was pink, and my fingernails cleaner than they had been in weeks. I washed my long hair.

Finally I emptied the tub, scrubbed the dirt from the sides of it, dried myself, and put on the nightdress she had left me. It was not night yet. Supper had been early, and though the sky was darkening because it was almost winter, and the oil lamps had been lit, it was not yet full night. I sat on the straight chair in the bathroom and waited. After a moment, the singing ended and Sister Jennie returned.

"I've set the girls to marking," she told me. "You can join them when we've combed your hair." I didn't even ask her what she meant by *marking*. It was just one more thing that I would have to learn.

I was tired, and confused by things, but I was not sad, not really. I was curious, and interested, and I liked the other girls, those I had met and talked to. Sister Jennie seemed very kind. If only she had not—

She tugged the comb through my hair gently, working out the snarls without hurting me, the way my mother always had. If only—

I just wish—

Oh, I do not know how to tell the rest! So I will simply say what happened next.

She saw my ring. "You'll need to give me that," she said, and held out her hand.

"My ring?" I asked. "Oh, no, it was my grand-mother's! My mother gave it to me on my birth-day," I explained. "I vowed never to take it off."

"Nay, you're a Shaker girl now, child," she said in her soft voice. "We Shakers do not ornament ourselves." She held out her hand for the ring.

I was accustomed to obeying, and so I began reluctantly to pull the ring from my finger. But I also began to cry. "Please," I begged, through my tears, "could I wear it just this one night? And then could I keep it in my drawer, so I could touch it now and then?"

She took it from me, and shook her head. "Nay," she said.

By now I was sobbing. I looked at her hand, her thin, undecorated hand, closed around my grandmother's ring. And my voice came out of me angry, a voice I hardly recognized as my own. "Nay!" I screamed at her. "Neigh! Neigh! You sound like a horse! You are a stupid horse with a big ugly face! Neigh!"

She didn't reply. She simply stood and took my arm and led me out of the bathroom and up the stairs. I was sobbing and saying rude things to her, but she was silent until we got to the room where my bed was. "You'll stay here until retiring time," she told me firmly.

She did one other thing before she left me there, seated on my bed. She took, from her pocket, a folded, ironed white handkerchief, and placed it in my lap. "Dry your tears, child," she said in a soft voice.

And I have. But my anger still burns in me, though it has lessened a bit as I have written and written—so many pages!—of these events.

So I am a Shaker girl now. My grandmother's ring is gone. And this is not my chosen land, and never will be.

Sunday, October 27, 1918

Five days have passed since I have written in my journal. It is difficult to find the time, for the days are so busy here. "Hands to work and hearts to God," the Shakers say. I am not at all sure where my heart is, but my hands have certainly been to work!

And to play, as well. Grace and Rebecca and Polly, the three who share the retiring room with me, have become my friends. Grace is full of energy and mischief. Polly, who wears glasses, is shy and scholarly. And Rebecca, with her blonde braids, reminds me a little of Emily Ann back in Portland, though Rebecca is quieter. Funny, but when it is dark, and we are in our beds, she talks a little more—exactly the time when we are not supposed to talk! We do whisper to each other a bit. Sometimes Sister Jennie has to come in and shush us. Isn't it odd, though, that we don't talk about the past? I know that Grace's mother died. But what of the others? What brought them here?

It is as if we are all starting fresh and new. But I suppose the other girls have sadnesses, too, and things they must put behind them, as I do. It seems those things must lie quiet within us all.

We have time to play when our work is finished each day. We run up and down the road playing tag with the other girls. We jump into the piles of raked leaves. Grace, who came in March, tells me that summer is the best. There is much to be done, then, in the gardens, of course. But there is time for fun. We can go over to the island in the millpond — Brother Isaac built a bridge — and there are swings there, and we can have picnics. The girls also have created a secret little place, Grace says, under the big stand of lilacs behind the girls' shop, and we will have tea parties there in summer.

Today is Sunday, the Sabbath, when we rest from work, attend worship, and do not play games of any sort, just read quietly or write—and that is why this afternoon I am able to take up my journal once more.

The weather is cool now, but not yet winter, of course. There are leaves everywhere on the ground, and we help to rake, though the boys do most of it. It must make them frustrated that we leap into their orderly piles and scatter leaves about. I have even seen Daniel at work with a rake! He never liked helping at home. But there are other boys here, and they work together. I've heard them laughing.

He wears a hat outdoors. All the boys and brethren do. But at mealtime the men and boys hang their hats on pegs in the waiting space (their waiting room is different, and they come in through a separate door. The brethren and boys even have their own staircase in the big dwelling!). With their hats off I am able to see that Daniel has a haircut. His hair is cut like the brethren, straight across in front, and makes him look older.

He looks at me now, sometimes. Just a glance.

When it is my turn to help in the kitchen, perhaps I will serve at the boys' table. I won't speak, of course. Meals are very silent. But if I get close to him, I will give him a smile so that he knows I am all right.

And I will be curious to see how he eats! At home, there were many vegetables that Daniel refused to eat. Parsnips were one. But here, vegetables are the main part of every dinner. And many parsnips! We are all supposed to "Shaker our plate," which means to eat everything and leave it perfectly clean. I don't find it difficult. I am always hungry at mealtime and the food is always good. But I am curious to see what Daniel does about parsnips!

I do notice that he kneels properly before meals, when we pray silently until Elder William says, "Amen." (All of us kneel, except the very elderly, who remain standing behind their chairs.) What Daniel says in prayer, of course, I cannot know. I myself have had a problem, not knowing what or how to pray here, and so I have just closed my eyes and knelt in silence. But Sister Jennie helped me with this when I opened my mind to her yesterday.

Now I must explain about opening one's mind.

It surprised me on Friday when Sister Jennie told me that confession was an important part of being a Shaker. I thought confession was only for Catholics, and I had finally figured out that Shakers weren't Catholics and Shaker sisters not nuns. But Friday night, when we girls were preparing to retire, Sister Jennie told me that I would be attending confession the next day.

"Is there a priest?" I asked, for I had not seen one anywhere.

But she laughed. "Nay," she said. "We Shakers have no priests, no pastors. We are all equal in our worship."

"My friend Marjorie always goes to her priest for confession," I told her. "She showed me how she crossed herself and said, 'Bless me, Father, for I have sinned.'"

Sister Jennie nodded. "Yea, we have all sinned," she told me, "and so we open our minds to one another. You will come to talk to me tomorrow, in the good room, after dinner."

The good room is across the front hall, in the girls' shop. There is a piano in it. I had peeked inside at the piano, for I have always wanted to learn to play the piano, but I had not yet been in the good room. And I was not sure I wanted to go there to talk to Sister Jennie, for although she had been kind to me all week, and treated me just as she treats the other girls, still there was the memory of the terrible night not long ago when I had screamed at her that she looked like a horse.

But I had no choice. One doesn't have a choice here. There are rules, and everyone follows them.

So yesterday, I went to her in the good room after the noon dinner. I'd rehearsed what I would say at confession. I planned to say very politely, "I am very sorry that I was so rude to you on my first night here, Sister Jennie. It will not happen again, I promise." I would get that over with first thing, and then I would change the subject and go on to my other sins, and there were many. I had spoken to Daniel because I didn't know the rule about boys and girls staying so separate. I had not finished my eggs at breakfast because the whites were too runny. And when we all knelt before meals to pray, I couldn't think what to say, so I sometimes just recited a nursery rhyme in my mind. I was quite sure that was a pretty serious sin, to be saying "Jack be nimble, Jack be quick" before the time came for "Amen."

Sister Jennie gestured to me to sit down in a chair in the good room, and she took her place on the sofa, facing me. I looked at the floor, took a deep breath, and was about to begin my confession with "I am very sorry —" but to my surprise, Sister Jennie spoke first.

"I am happy to have you in our family, Lydia," she said.

I looked up at her. How could she be happy to have someone as rude and ungrateful as me? But I could see she was not just being polite. She really felt it.

"Do you know," she went on, "we have forty-eight head of cattle here at Sabbathday Lake?"

I shook my head. "Sometimes I see my brother, Daniel, out in the field with the cows," I told her. "But I didn't know there were forty-eight."

"Ten swine," she went on, "and a pair of mules."

"Oh," I replied. Who would have guessed that confession consisted of a listing of the farm animals?

"Two draft horses. Those are the very big, sturdy ones. Two driving horses. Eldress Lizzie, elderly as she is, can drive the team—imagine! She's the only sister who can do that.

"And then," Sister Jennie added, "we have one very old horse." She smiled. "I've always been fond of horses. They have sweet faces, I think."

I began to cry suddenly. "I'm so sorry," I said through my tears. "So, so sorry! I didn't mean it, Sister Jennie! Really I didn't! Truly I don't think you look like a horse! I was just so scared, and feeling so sorry for myself! And then you took my grandmother's ring! And—"

"I understand," she said. "And the time will come when you'll understand, too, Lydia. You'll begin Sunday School tomorrow, here in this room, with the other girls. You'll learn about our beliefs. Simplicity is one of our very important values. We don't ornament ourselves."

I looked at her, at her dark, long-sleeved dress, her unrouged face, her hair pulled back beneath the net cap. I could see the goodness in her because it shone through the plainness. I stopped crying, and once again she passed me a handkerchief.

She chuckled. "You know each of our girls learns the various jobs in the community. 'Hands to work and hearts to God,' we say. I think we'll start you helping in the laundry," she said. "Then you'll think twice about using so many handkerchiefs!"

I laughed with her as I wiped my eyes. "Sister Jennie?" I said.

"Yea?"

"This is really, truly a confession. When we kneel in the dining room, I don't know what to pray."

"You can use the words that Mother Ann

taught. 'I pray God bless me, and give me grace, and make me a good child.'"

I repeated the words, then said, "That's all?"

Sister Jennie smiled. "Amen," she said. "Ah, child, that's everything."

She rose, and I knew confession was over. Or, as she called it, opening one's mind.

Monday, October 28, 1918

School has reopened. The teacher is Sister Cora Soule, who is quite stern.

We girls all walked together across the road to the schoolhouse. I was wearing a new dress that Sister Jennie had made for me! She has a sewing machine at her end of the large room in the girls' shop, and she sews when we are gathered there working on our own handwork. She even asked me which color I would like, from her collection of fabrics, and I chose blue. I wore it with a knitted blue sweater from the closet. I wondered who else had worn that sweater. Nothing seems to belong just to us—even my bed, as they told me when I arrived, had been Eliza's bed. I do not know what happened to Eliza, but perhaps she ran away, or died. And maybe this was her sweater!

At Sunday School, studying Mother Ann's teachings, we learn that everything belongs to all of us. It is why, that first day, Sister Jennie took *The Secret Garden* from me and put it on the shelf with the other books. "Community of goods," it is called, and it is one of our beliefs.

(Well, it is one of the Shaker beliefs. I am not at all sure that it is mine.)

But the blue dress, with its white collar, is mine. Sister Jennie made it just for me.

To my amazement, the boys also came to school! In the old days, boys went to school in winter and girls in summer. But now we all go together, though we don't speak to each other, and we sit on different sides of the room — the boys' desks are on the south side of the huge woodstove, and the girls' on the north. We have different recess times. We have different bookshelves, boys and girls. The girls' shelf has *Little Women*, I can see. I do not know what books the boys' shelf has, but I know one boy who will not be reading them. That is Daniel, my brother. Daniel does not like to read.

There were other children. I had never seen them before. They were dressed differently, and one of the girls had a fancy hair ribbon. At the beginning of the school day, after we said the Lord's Prayer and the Pledge of Allegiance (there is a large flag in the schoolroom, and another outside), Sister Cora introduced me because I was new. She said each child's name and explained that Louise and Marian (the one with the hair ribbon) and Gloria were from the world. One of the boys was, too.

I was from the world such a very short time ago, and already it seems like a foreign place!

"Lydia, what grade were you in before you came here?" the teacher asked.

"Sixth," I said. "I had just started sixth."

"You'll sit here with Polly, then," she said. Each desk had room for two, so I took my place beside Polly. Of course I already knew her because she shares the retiring room with Grace and Rebecca and me. She smiled at me when I sat down beside her.

I whispered, "There's my brother, Daniel, over there." I pointed. Polly looked confused. Sister Cora glared at me for whispering, and Daniel glared at me for calling attention to him. So I simply stared at the maps on the wall and pretended to be very, very interested in ancient Greece.

The dinner bell rang just before noon. Sister Cora's meal was delivered to her by one of the kitchen sisters so that she could stay with the children from the world while they ate the lunches they had brought from home. The rest of us all walked back across the road to the dwelling house for our dinner. This time, when we knelt, I remembered the words of Mother Ann Lee's prayer that Sister Jennie had taught me. *I pray God bless me, and give me grace, and make me a good child.*

Monday is always laundry day. The laundry is on the ground floor of the sisters' shop, behind the house where I live with the other girls. The sisters stand facing each other at big tubs and scrub the clothing on washboards, but the larger things, like sheets, are all washed in an amazing huge machine, which is filled with water and contains wooden slats that move back and forth by an electric motor. They tell me that the Shakers invented this machine and that they have invented many things — even clothespins!

After the washing, the large things had to be rinsed, and Rebecca and I had the task of swishing them in clear water with wooden poles. From there they went through a wringer and into a basket to be hung to dry. We worked, hanging things, after breakfast until time for school. From the schoolhouse windows, and when I walked to the dining room for dinner, I could see the sheets billowing in the cold breeze. After school, in the late afternoon, Rebecca and I went back to take things from the line and fold them. Grace came along to help.

This was my first job in the Shaker village: laundry. But it would not last long, I was told. All jobs change often, so that one never becomes disheartened by doing something too long, and so that we learn to do everything.

I am looking forward to helping the sisters make candy! They do it in a special room in the sisters' shop, and pack it into lovely boxes to sell. I suppose that those who work there have a chance to nibble.

But for now, my job is laundry. Tomorrow is Tuesday. On Tuesday, they tell me, we iron.

Tuesday, October 29, 1918

I hate ironing.

I suppose at my next confession, when I open my mind to Sister Jennie, I will have to tell her that I hate something. Shakers don't hate.

And she will explain to me once more about the Shaker way, how our work is a way of creating heaven here on earth. That is why we make everything spotlessly clean, and take joy in doing it. But do we have to make everything perfectly flat, as well? Think of all the ways we use handkerchiefs! They end up damp and crumpled. Why should we iron them at the start?

That is my job. Ironing handkerchiefs. It is how young girls start learning.

I burned myself twice today. In a room above the laundry, we iron at big tables that have been covered over with cloth. The irons are all inside the enormous oven, which is heated by the fire below. We change them, taking new hot ones as the ones we are using turn cool. The older sisters do it so easily, so quickly — they are working on the larger things, sheets mostly, and the brethren's shirts — that I did not see a single sister burn herself. But I did, twice! A very nice sister named Hazel went and got me some cooling salve for my burned hand. But no one seemed to feel very sorry for me, even though I cried a little from the pain. It is part of learning, they told me; they have all been through it, and soon it will be easier for me.

Rebecca, who is helping in the laundry with me this week, will soon be moving on to a different job, probably in the kitchen. I like Rebecca, though not as much as I like Grace, because Rebecca is very serious. She answers questions in school very seriously, and walks to dinner very seriously, and she even irons as if it were a very serious job. I know that Rebecca has never said a nursery rhyme in place of a prayer. Grace is more fun. Grace giggles and causes mischief. She can make her eyes cross toward her nose without even holding a finger up for them to aim at. She does it in the schoolroom when the teacher's back is turned.

Here is one good thing about working in the laundry. I can listen to the other sisters talking to each other. They forget that I am there, I think.

That is how I learned about Pearl and Lillian Beckwith, two of the younger girls in the girls' shop. Their mother brought them to the Shakers a year ago because she couldn't care for them. Imagine that! How sad they must have been! But then, a few months later, she came and asked for them back.

"Couldn't live without them," I heard one of the sisters explain. "Or so she said."

So off they went again, with their mother, those two little girls. I felt happy for them when I heard that. My mother can never come back for me. But I wondered: Why are they here, then, living in the girls' shop, sleeping in the room next to mine (the little one wets her bed! Sister Jennie is trying to help her get over that affliction) if their mother couldn't live without them, if she came and got them?

It is because she brought them back again just last month. Once again she had not been able to take care of them properly. "Poor little things," the sister said. "They were so dirty and ragged."

(I wonder what they thought of me when I arrived!)

"And sick," another sister remembered.

They all nodded. The little one, especially. So very sick. "I thought sure she'd be entering the spirit life."

That is what they call dying. I like it, in a way. I like thinking of my parents and little Lucy being in the spirit life. It doesn't scare me, as dying does.

I kept listening as I pressed my iron on handkerchief after handkerchief, folding each one carefully. (They were right, that after a while it becomes easier.) I wanted to hear more about Pearl and Lillian, how they had gotten clean and well and happy in such a short time. How is it they are able to eat their dinner? How do they sit in the front room at the girls' shop and listen to stories, working on their fancywork, smiling at *The Five Little Peppers*, and all the time knowing that their mother doesn't want them anymore?

But the sisters began talking of someone else, someone named Ruth. "Been here since she was nine," I heard a sister say.

"Not one word of thanks," another added. "Just up and left. After fourteen years."

They all made small disapproving sounds. The sisters do not speak badly of anyone. Never once have I heard them do so. But I could tell that they were troubled. Partly by Ruth's leaving, but also by the fact that she never thanked them for the fourteen years of her growing up: for their food, for their teaching, for their clothes. For their prayers.

I added it up in my mind. Whoever she was — Ruth — she had been 23 years old. I wondered where she went.

Then someone spoke of Emma Freeman, who had left in early July, wanting to be part of the world. But a month later she was back. I know who Emma is. She helps serve the food at dinner. It seemed amazing to me that she had gone away, been disappointed, returned, and now does her job with the kind of attention and diligence that all the sisters have. They all look as if they have never undergone a single change in their lives. But I see it isn't true. Each one has her own story.

"So you can leave!" I startled myself by saying the thought aloud.

The chubby one, Sister Lavinia, was changing her iron. She looked at me and chuckled. "Did you think we are all captives, child?" she asked me.

I felt myself blushing. "No," I said. "I just don't quite understand how it works."

It was late afternoon by then, almost time to finish the ironing, put the things away, tidy up, and ready ourselves for dinner. While I made my way through the rest of my small pile of hankies, Rebecca working silently near me, the sisters talked about their own lives. How they had chosen this life, the Shaker life, and signed what they call the covenant. Some of them, the younger ones, still teenagers, had not reached the time of choosing yet.

I listened as they talked of their happiness as Shakers.

I still hate ironing. But I am coming to like the sisters.

Friday, November 1, 1918

Sister Jennie came to me this evening after supper, when I was working on my horrible knitting. I can't do a single row without a mistake. She has me making a washcloth—the absolutely simplest knitting project there is. Just a square, that's all. Even little Lillian, the smallest child in the girls' shop, makes washcloths perfectly. But again and again I drop stitches, or twist them. Once I had my square almost finished, I thought, and I showed it to Sister Jennie. But she pointed out a place where I had knitted two stitches together by mistake, way back in the first rows. "Rip it out back to there, and start in again," she told me.

"But it doesn't matter! It's just a silly washcloth!" I argued. "You can still scrub your face with it, even with that tiny mistake!"

Sister Jennie smiled. She has told me this so often. "We Shakers strive for perfection," she reminded me, "even in a silly washcloth. It's how—"

"I know." I sighed. "It's how we create heaven on earth." Secretly I thought that I would enjoy a heaven with lumpy washcloths.

This evening, though, she didn't even ask to see my knitting. She told me that she had arranged a meeting with my brother on Sunday.

"The brethren feel it may be a help to him, to visit with you," she told me. "Daniel is a little . . ."

I could tell that she couldn't think of what word to use. Father—or Uncle Henry—would have had a string of words for him: lazy, ungrateful, disrespectful. Mother would have been more soothing. He's young, she would say. He needs time to grow. He's a good boy, down deep.

"He's a little confused," I told Sister Jennie, "and he hates school."

She chuckled. She knows that. Sister Jennie helps Sister Cora often at the school, and sees

Daniel, how he stares out the window when he should be working on his papers.

"But when I needed him," I told her, "he was there. He was the one who called Uncle Henry. He put his arms around me when we realized . . ."

I couldn't go on, but she knew what I meant. When our family was gone.

"He just needs time," I suggested.

"Yea. Some do. Especially boys. You talk to him Sunday, Lydia, and see if you can cheer him a bit."

I told her I would try. And I felt inside the pocket of my dress, where I carry my little family of stones with me. The ragged-edge one that I called my brother was there, big and out of place beside the others. I smoothed its edge with my finger, but it was jagged and rough still, no matter how I tried to make it fit comfortably with the rest.

There is one other little stone in the group now, too. A smallish one that Grace and I picked up in the road just beyond the schoolhouse. She was wearing a purple dress, and suddenly she leaned down and picked up a stone the exact same shade. "Look!" she said. "A little stone wearing my dress!"

Till then I hadn't told a single soul about my stone family. It was my private, secret thing. But something made me tell Grace that morning, during the school recess. I showed her how I kept them in my pocket, and at night under my pillow. I told her how they made me feel less lonely. I knew Grace had lost her own mother. That's why she was here with the Shakers.

"You could make a stone family, too," I told her.

I could see her thinking about that. Then, to my surprise, she handed me the purple stone. "Could I be in yours?" she asked.

Part of me wanted to say no, that it was just us, Walter and Caroline Pierce and their three children. But I looked at Grace, usually so lively and laughing, and now, suddenly, she was quite solemn. I didn't know anything about her family, beyond the mother who had died last March. But I could see that her memories were making her sad. So I said yes, and took the purple stone and added it to my little group. The school bell rang then. Running back to the schoolhouse door, I felt the stones shift and settle in my pocket. Grace glanced at me and smiled.

Saturday, November 2, 1918

I like Saturdays here. They remind me of home.

In the morning, we clean. Our retiring room, the room I share with Grace, Rebecca, and Polly, is swept and tidied and we put clean linens on our beds. Each girl straightens the drawers in which she keeps her things. At home, I had my own room. Here I share with the other girls, so there is no privacy. But on Saturday mornings we work together. After we finish our own room, we help the smaller girls, whose rooms are across the hall. There is always a lot of laughter.

Sister Jennie has a separate room on the second floor, and she cleans hers as well. No maids, no hired girls, among the Shakers! "Sweeping the devil out!" she says, as she pushes the broom to the doorway.

On the third floor, the older girls busy themselves as well. Once I thought the mysterious Eliza, whose bed I now sleep in, had run away or died. Not so! Eliza is on the third floor now. She and the girls there are twelve and thirteen. When they leave the girls' shop, as they begin to be women, they move across to the large dwelling, where Second Eldress Prudence Stickney is in charge of the younger sisters and the teen-aged girls. But for now they are still girls, and from the third floor come giggles as they tidy their rooms.

And after the cleaning, we all gather downstairs in the large room where each evening we do our handwork. But on Saturday mornings it is mending. Mostly darning stockings! I once watched my mother do that. Now I have to learn to do it myself, and it is tiresome. This morning I found myself scolding little Lillian for being so rough on her clothing, and especially her stockings, as she plays outdoors. She had torn a hole in one knee by climbing the trees behind the girls' shop! And I was the one who had to mend it. Her fingers are still too young and awkward.

"Soon enough there won't be much playing outdoors," Sister Jennie reminded us. She was at her sewing machine at the far end of the big room. This morning she was stitching some underthings. "It'll snow before long."

We all looked through the windows at the sky. In October it had been so blue, and the trees golden. But now the leaves are falling faster and faster. The ash trees are already bare. And the sky is gray.

"Sometimes the snow is so deep that we can't leave the house," one of the older girls said. "Last winter we were here for two whole days until the boys shoveled us out! They brought our food to us so we didn't starve. But they had to get the way to the barn cleared first, so they could tend the animals."

"Yea, but after it was all shoveled," Eliza added, "Elder William took us on a sleigh ride!"

A sleigh ride! I have never been on one. Now I am hoping for snow *soon*.

After cleaning and mending and dinner, we can play for all of Saturday afternoon. In bad weather, we will be able to use the games and books in the big room here. But we like outdoors best. This afternoon the other girls and I climbed up to the tippy-top of the hill behind the meetinghouse and school, and rolled down! We got burrs stuck in our sweaters and stockings, and dried grass in our hair. But it was such fun.

From the top of the hill we could look down on the Shaker village, the buildings gleaming white in the November light, and the large pink brick one in their midst. It was like a toy town. The lake beyond was dark gray, and the pines around it deep green. In the fields behind the barn we could see the cattle, like miniature figures, and the men and boys at work. No play for them on Saturdays!

For a moment I stood there on the hilltop with my arms spread wide, my hair blown every which way by the wind. I thought of my mother and knew somehow that she would smile to see me here. I watched as the other girls, giggling, threw themselves all atumble one by one down the hill. Some geese flew overhead, heading south. Suddenly I remembered the words in one of the Shaker hymns we had been learning in the evenings:

Oh, the blessings rich and many,
Which are mine to share today!

Then I followed the other girls and flung myself onto the high, brown grass and tumbled, rolling and laughing, down toward Sabbathday Lake.

Sunday, November 3, 1918

Sundays are very different from Saturdays. We can sleep a little later, and we dress in our best clothes. Of course for me that means something else out of the big closet. But there are lots of dresses to choose from. Today I wore a dark blue dress with a lace collar. It fit nicely and made me feel pretty, but I remembered the clothes I once had, especially a pink dress with smocking and embroidery. All of those things were left behind in Portland, and I suppose they have been given away. Some other girl may be wearing my pink dress now. Or perhaps they have been destroyed because they were in a house contaminated by the sickness. I think I would rather have my pink dress burned than given to another girl. It is a selfish thought, I know.

The influenza is still raging in Maine. But we have not been afflicted here at Sabbathday Lake, at least not by the epidemic. Many children were sick before I arrived, but the doctor said it was not the flu. And they all got well. Dr. Sturgis comes from time to time to tend Sister Gertrude and Eldress Lizzie for their heart trouble. But most small ailments are treated by the herbs grown here in summer. The sisters package the dried herbs and sell them to the world, and they are much in demand. It will be one of my jobs, I suppose, to help with the packaging of herbs, and I will like it much better than ironing!

Dressed in our Sunday dresses, we march in line into the chapel in the dwelling house. The sisters are already in place, and we girls sit on benches in the back. We are all completely quiet. After a bit, the Eldresses enter through the sisters' entrance and then, after a moment, just as the clock strikes ten, the door of the brothers' entrance opens and

Elder William enters, followed by the brethren and the boys, including Daniel.

Sister Mamie Curtis plays the organ and there is a lot of singing, with Bible reading in between the songs. The Shakers have many, many songs. We sometimes sing in the evenings, and gradually we will learn the songs. Though there are hymnbooks in the chapel, most of the sisters never need to look.

I like the singing part. All the girls do. But the Bible reading goes on for a very long time, and then Elder William gives a talk that seems to take forever. We must sit very straight, hands folded in our laps, and not wiggle or fidget. Lillian has trouble—she is so young—so Sister Jennie sits beside her and reminds her firmly, with a touch, to be still.

There are times of silence, too, for us to think about the readings and the Elder's words. Then the meeting is "open to the spirit" and sisters rise and speak. We girls do not do this, but Sister Jennie has told us that next week we are to recite some scripture at the Sabbath meeting. I am already a little nervous about that.

There is one other thing that makes me — well, not nervous exactly. But startled. I was accustomed to prayers at my church back home. "Our Father, who art in heaven" — I've said that as long as I can remember.

But the Shakers pray not to Our Father, but to Father-Mother God. It is always that — Father-Mother — never Father alone. They believe in a God that is male and female both! Isn't that odd?

After what seems a very long time, we march out silently, the children last. I tried this morning to catch Daniel's eye, to smile at him, but he did not look my way. It is the same at meals, and in school. Of course the girls do not converse with the boys in school or any other place. But still, I keep hoping that Daniel will glance at me, or even grin the way he used to, with his mischievous smile. He was once, despite his often imperfect behavior — his willfulness, as my mother called it — a cheerful boy. Now his face seems a mask, with no expression, and I wondered, during meeting, what we would say to each other at our visit this afternoon.

Sunday School is held in the good room on the first floor, the room with the piano, after dinner on Sunday. We have changed out of our best dresses by then, and sit on the scratchy horsehair sofa and chairs in that room while Sister Jennie instructs us about the Bible and the teachings of Mother Ann Lee, who was the founder of the Shakers. I used to wonder who they meant when they referred to "Mother." "Mother teaches us to clean our room well because there is no dirt in heaven." "Mother says to take good care of what you have and provide places for your things." Those are the kinds of things that Sister Jennie tells us, and I had found myself thinking: Whose mother? Jennie's mother? My mother? How would Sister Jennie know what my mother had said?

But it is Mother Ann Lee she means, and whose teachings we must learn and follow.

Today Sister Jennie talked about pacifism. Shakers will not go to war. The brothers here at Sabbathday Lake were required to register for the draft, but if they were called to duty they would not bear arms. During the War between the States,

Elder Frederick Evans went to President Lincoln and talked to him, and finally the president agreed that they would not have to fight, though it pained him.

Listening to her turned my thoughts again to Daniel. One time Daniel had told me that he would lie about his age and join the army. Soon, though, there will be no war for him to go to. I heard the sisters in the laundry say that the war will soon be over and the killing will end.

Oh, my dear brother!

I am writing this after Sunday School. On Sunday afternoons we may do what we like, but no work and no play. What else is left? I read, or take a walk, or write in my journal. But today, very soon, I am to have a visit with my brother.

Later

Sister Jennie came to get me to take me to my visit with Daniel. Another girl, Elvira, had a visit with her grandparents, and came with us to the big dwelling. Elvira went to one of the sitting rooms, and we could see her there with an elderly couple who hugged her. One of the older sisters went into that room and sat with them while they visited. Sister Jennie stayed with me and we waited in a front room for Daniel.

It seemed so strange. Not long ago, Daniel and I lived in the same house. We sat at the same table for meals, and laughed and argued. We walked together, sometimes, to school. We quarreled a lot, that is true, in earlier days. But during those last days when we tended our parents and sister, we worked almost as one person. There was no time to argue, no need for it. We were desperate to make things right, if we could. And when we failed, we wept together.

Now we must behave as if we are strangers. I may not speak to him at meals, or during school. He lives in the building behind the brick dwelling, above the boys' shop, where they learn woodworking, tinware, shoemaking, and other things.

"Did you have any brothers, Sister Jennie?" I asked suddenly, as we waited there. "I don't mean the brethren. I mean — well, you know: a real brother."

She shook her head. "Nay."

"A husband?" I asked, amazing myself because I knew it was a rude question.

But she laughed. "Oh, my," she said. "Nay. I came here as a child. And you know Shakers don't marry! It's part of Mother's teaching."

"But didn't you want to? Don't the others want to?"

She shook her head. "It would take from the community, to have special attachments like that."

I know that is why we mustn't talk to the boys, why the sisters and brethren avoid each other, even using separate staircases. There is to be no special affection developing. I remembered from my school days, from my time in the world, as I was now thinking of my life with my first family, how girls and boys teased each other, sometimes smiled at ones who were a little special. There was a boy in my class at school. His name was Edward. I thought him quite handsome. Once I gave him some cookies I'd brought from home. It wasn't courting, not really. We were too young. But it was maybe the beginning of—

My thoughts were interrupted when Daniel appeared at the door. One of the brethren had brought him. He gestured to my brother to go into the room; then he turned and left.

"Hello, Daniel," Sister Jennie said. "I've brought Lydia to have a little visit with you."

He sat awkwardly on the settee. Usually when I saw him at meals he was wearing his work clothes, overalls and heavy shoes. But today, Sunday, he wore his Sunday trousers and ironed shirt, the same clothes he had worn at this morning's meeting. Perhaps in his pocket he had a handkerchief ironed by me.

"I can't stay long," he said. "I have to help with milking soon."

Of course some farm chores couldn't have a day of rest.

"Do you like the animals?" I asked him. "I went with Sister Caroline once to help feed the chickens and gather eggs, but it was so noisy, and they pecked at me."

I could see him start to smile. He was probably picturing me shrieking when the chickens ran at me and pecked. He knows what a coward I sometimes am.

"I like the cows," he said. "There's one heifer, though, that's bad tempered."

"Her name should be Frances Dudley," I suggested, and Daniel grinned. Mrs. Dudley had been our neighbor, who complained loudly about everything and criticized her husband all the time.

Sister Jennie was sitting very quietly, working on a little piece of embroidery. Hands to work and heart to God. The Shaker sisters call embroidery "marking," and I will have to learn soon, to mark. If I ever finish my knitted washcloth!

"Brother Delmer wants me to help him with the apple packing after school tomorrow," Daniel said.

"They say it was a good crop this year," I replied. Daniel nodded. The orchards are across the road. I had heard the sisters say there are 800 bushels of apples stored in the cellar, now, already this fall.

"Remember what Uncle Henry said about

the Shaker apples, before we ever knew what the Shakers were?"

But Daniel didn't reply. I suppose he didn't want to be reminded of Uncle Henry.

Uncle Henry had said that you could always be certain, with a crate of Shaker apples, that the ones on the bottom would be as good as the ones on the top. No hiding of bruised ones.

It is because of Brother Delmer and his study of orchards that we have such fine apples, not only to sell, but also for the pies and applesauce that we eat here at Sabbathday Lake. One evening not long ago, many of us worked together on the cutting and drying of apple pieces, and they are stored away now for the months to come.

Daniel and I sat there for a few minutes, talking aimlessly of the McIntoshes and Cortlands, of the animals, the weather, and the price of eggs. (Last winter Shaker eggs brought 68 cents a dozen, but by spring it was down to 38 cents. It is a worry to the community.) Sister Jennie's fingers moved meticulously on the small piece of cloth she was marking with blue thread.

Then the brother appeared again in the doorway and motioned to Daniel that it was time for the visit to end. I could hear Elvira saying goodbye to her grandparents across the hall. Sister Jennie folded her embroidery and rose.

Suddenly Daniel came across the room toward my chair and I was terrified that he was going to touch me, maybe give me a hug, something so strictly forbidden. But he didn't. Instead he set a small wooden box on the table beside my chair.

"I made this," he said awkwardly.

I looked at Sister Jennie, and she nodded that I might have it.

"Thank you," I said to my brother, and then he was gone. We could hear the door of the dwelling close behind him and the brother who accompanied him.

"All the boys learn to work with wood," Sister Jennie explained.

I carried the box back to the girls' shop, half listening as Elvira chattered about her grandparents, how her grandmother suffered so with sciatica but was getting some relief from a new pill.

"And look!" Elvira said happily. "They brought us this!" She held up a small bag and handed it to Sister Jennie. "Candies! Enough for each of us!"

Sister Jennie smiled. "We'll have them after supper. It was good of them, Elvira."

"Last time," Elvira explained to me, knowing I was new, "they brought me a doll. But I couldn't keep it because the other girls didn't have them. We can only have things that are for us all."

I nodded. She didn't need to explain that. My book had been taken from me for the same reason. But at least we are all enjoying hearing *The Secret Garden* read aloud, now that we have finished *The Five Little Peppers*, though I always feel a little moment of resentment when Sister Jennie picks it up in the evening and turns to the page where she left off last. *It's mine*, I think. But it is a bad way of thinking. A worldly way. I will confess it when the time comes again to open my mind.

But she had let me keep my journal. And now, too, the little box that Daniel made. I thought that I would put my little family of stones into it. It was only when I began to do that, sitting on my bed after supper, before going downstairs for our evening singing and prayers (and a chapter of *The Secret Garden*), that I lifted its lid and realized there was a folded piece of paper inside. Daniel had written me a note.

"I AM LEAVING SOON," it said. "DO NOT WORRY ABOUT ME."

Sunday, November 10, 1918

This morning, at the Sabbath meeting, was the morning that we girls were to say our verses of scripture. I had selected one and memorized it and practiced it all week. But last evening I changed my mind and chose another. This morning I stood and said it aloud with no mistakes.

A friend loveth at all times, and a brother is born for adversity. Proverbs 17:17.

I think I saw some of the brethren smile a little at its words. But it did not make me smile. It made me think about Daniel. It made me sad.

Monday, November 11, 1918

It has been hard to write anything. I have worried so about Daniel, about whether I should tell someone about his note. Keeping secrets is not the Shaker way. But what would happen to my brother if I told? So I did nothing. Just worried.

Each day last week Daniel was there in school, staring through the window as he always does. I could see him out in the schoolyard at boys' recess, near the wall around the Shaker cemetery, talking to the farm boy from the world. They were laughing together at something.

He was at meeting yesterday, same as always, sitting with the other boys. I watched him when I said my piece of scripture—I don't think he was listening—and while we sang the Shaker songs. Here is one:

> *Hop up and jump up and whirl 'round,*
> *whirl 'round,*
> *Gather love, here it is, all 'round, all 'round.*
> *Here is love flowing 'round,*
> *Catch it as you whirl 'round.*

Reach up and reach down,
Here it is all 'round.

The songs are so different from what we sang at Woodfords Congregational Church: "Fairest Lord Jesus" and the like. And hopping and jumping and whirling? Well! That is because in the past, the Shakers actually did that as part of their worship. Quivering and trembling in their religious excitement: that is how they became known as Shakers! They say that people came from many miles to watch a Shaker service and the dancing, in the old days. But that is no longer true. No dancing anymore, no shaking or whirling.

This morning in the laundry (it is Monday, wash day, once again), when I was scrubbing handkerchiefs at the washboard (scraping my knuckles!), Sister Helen was reaching up and down into the huge tub where she rinsed the wet linens in clear water after they had come from the washing machine. It made me think of the song. *"Reach up and reach down,"* I found myself singing aloud, and Sister Helen heard me and began to laugh. She was the one who explained about the dancing.

"All of them in line, brethren and sisters," she said. "It must have been something to see."

"Why did you stop dancing?" I asked her.

Sister Helen knotted her brow. "The older Shakers began to be infirm," she explained. "Have you noticed how, at prayers before meals, the older Shakers stand instead of kneeling?"

I nodded. There are many older Shakers. I knew that Dr. Sturgis had recently come to see Sister Gertrude and Eldress Lizzie for their hearts. Some of the others seem a little stooped, and frail.

"Earthly bodies wear out," she said in a kindly voice. "It's hard for some of them to kneel now."

She maneuvered a large, rinsed sheet through the wringer attached to the tub and then went to hang it with clothes pegs on the indoor line where laundry dries in bad weather. "More and more, it was only the younger ones who could do the dancing. And it is our way, you know, that everything be shared. So as time passed, the younger Shakers stopped feeling the spirit and the gift for dancing, too. Now we are all able to worship together in the same way."

"I wish I could have seen it," I told her.

Sister Helen called to some of the other sisters who were folding clothing at the big table. "Lydia wonders what the Shaker dancing looked like!" she called.

"*Reach up and reach down,*" Sister Edith sang aloud, gesturing to the sheet on the line, and the one waiting below in a basket.

"*Hop up and jump up,*" sang Sister Hannah from the washtub, and did a tiny hop.

And suddenly, without any discussion, the three laundry workers, in their Shaker dresses and aprons and caps, formed a line and performed the song and the dance, making the gestures and postures, the small hops and jumps that went with the words.

They invited me to join in and we all did it a second time.

"*Gather love, here it is, all 'round, all 'round,*" we sang loudly, making the gathering motions with our arms.

It made me forget my bleeding knuckles and the endless stack of hankies waiting to be scrubbed. When I went back to the washboard, I felt renewed and full of energy. And loved. I felt loved.

At mealtime we received the news that the war was over. We said special prayers of thanksgiving that the cruel battles had ended and the young men would come home now to their families. I found myself thinking again of Daniel. At least he cannot join up and go to war. So perhaps he will change his mind about leaving.

Tuesday, November 12, 1918

I was mistaken in my hopes. Daniel is gone. He crept away during the night and was not there in the boys' shop this morning when the waking bell rang. At dinner, Elder William spoke of it in his prayer, and asked the Lord to protect a willful boy and keep him safe from harm and from the world's dangers. I closed my eyes very tight and echoed the prayer in my mind.

Monday, December 2, 1918

It is three weeks since Daniel disappeared in the night. No one speaks of him. Nothing has changed, but his chair is still there, empty at meals and meeting. The days continue much the same as always, with school and work and meals and prayer.

I have not written in my journal in all this time.

I am no longer in the laundry but in the kitchen, helping Sister Sirena. Some of the older girls help here, too, the teenagers who live in the big dwelling and wear the Shaker dress but are not yet true Shakers. One of them, Ida, has eyes for a boy who comes with a delivery wagon. The sisters are worried about it. They speak firmly to her and bid her stay inside when the delivery boy comes with his goods. I have heard that it has happened before, a girl running off with a boy, though no one will tell me the details. I think she married him. And perhaps Ida, too, wants to marry a boy of the world and have a family.

It makes me remember my parents. My mother had told me of how she met my father at a church gathering, and he came to court her, and took her to a concert, once. Her parents said she must finish high school, so she worked very hard to graduate early, and completely gave up her plans of going on to teachers' college because she wanted to marry Walter Pierce, who had deep blue eyes and a promising future. She was only eighteen when they were married at Woodfords Congregational Church. She wore my grandmother's wedding dress and carried white lilacs. She pressed some blossoms in her Bible, and showed them to me once, all brown and fragile, the lilac smell gone. There was a reception in the church parlor, with lemon cakes.

My mother was 34 when she died, but I think she had a happy life and many hopes. I vow to make her proud of me.

I wonder if she would want me to marry and have children, as she did. Or would she admire the Shaker sisters, who give their love to Mother Ann and to the orphans they tend and teach?

I do not think the delivery boy much of a catch. He has unkempt hair and blemished skin, and his nails are dirty. I hope Ida does not go off with him. She is a good student and could go on, they say, to college and perhaps become the teacher here at Sabbathday Lake when Sister Cora grows too old. Even if she signs the covenant and becomes a true Shaker, Ida could do that. The Shaker teachers go to the Normal School during summer to keep their credentials.

But if she were to go off with the delivery boy, I fear she would live in poverty and never have a real chance at a happy and contented life. I watch her rolling our pie crust and wonder what she is thinking about. Sometimes she grins at me as if we share a joke.

I have an idea. Maybe the delivery boy knows where Daniel has gone. If I could only find a way to ask him!

Or the farm boy who attends our school? Perhaps he knows. He and Daniel talked and laughed at recess time.

I can see the pastures from the kitchen

windows. One of those cows is the bad-tempered heifer that Daniel liked best. I'm sure she knows where he is. He must have leaned his head into her side on chilly mornings and told her his secrets.

Sunday, December 8, 1918

> *O pray for the fathers, the sisters, and brothers,*
> *O pray for the whole household,*
> *O pray for the mothers, remember all others;*
> *O pray for the whole, whole world.*

This was a song we sang today at worship. I have decided that perhaps if I write down the words of the songs, I will learn and remember them more quickly. The sisters and brethren seem to know every song—and there are hundreds—but I stumble along and forget. Today's was easy, though, and meaningful for me. I prayed for my parents, and my little sister, that they are content in the spirit world, and for Daniel, who is just as lost to me as they are. As for the "whole, whole world"? Well, it will have to get along without my prayers, for I have so many others to concentrate on. The household? That would be this little village, I think, this little village of Shakers. And yes, I will pray for them, though I expect they do not need my prayers, for they are nothing but good.

Except, perhaps, for Ida. The other sisters in the kitchen are very put out with Ida. They try to be charitable but I can hear them murmuring about how she spends entirely too much time smoothing her hair and pinching her cheeks to make them pink, always when the delivery boy is expected. I wonder if she talks about the delivery boy in confession.

Monday, December 9, 1918

I almost forgot to say that finally I have nearly finished knitting my washcloth! Day after day I have tortured the yarn into knots and snarls, and then Sister Jennie directs me to take it all apart and begin again and again. But now, suddenly, I realize it is beginning to form a perfect square, and with no mistakes! And I can see for the first time what she meant when she said we must always work toward perfection. Toward a heaven here on earth.

I expect one doesn't need a washcloth in heaven! But it does feel heavenly to look at that little square with each stitch the right size, all in order, all in line.

Wednesday, December 11, 1918

The first snow! Later this year than usual, and just a few inches, not enough to close school. But the roads are treacherous, and so Brother Delmer has had to cancel a trip to Portland. He was going to take Eldress Lizzie to the special doctor she sees for her ears. They go in the automobile! The electric, they call it, though it is officially a Selden. It has already driven 32,000 miles. Brother Delmer is the only one to drive it, and once, last spring, the mule team had to go and pull him out when he was stuck in some mud.

But today the electric stays in the lower garage (which Brother Delmer built especially to house it) and Eldress Lizzie's ears will have to wait. The brethren and boys are all out shoveling.

When I went to the kitchen after school, there were extra pots to wash, because there were two kinds of hot soup at dinner, and cocoa as well. Everyone's cheeks are pink with the cold, and we girls are wrapped in thick knitted scarves to keep our ears and necks warm.

(I wonder if someday I will be able to knit a scarf! I can't even seem to complete a foolish little square washcloth! Last evening, when I thought it was almost finished, and I was feeling so accomplished, I had to rip out two rows. Again!)

Snow makes me think about Christmas. At home, before the epidemic that changed everything, we would be busy making gifts and cookies for the holidays.

Last year Mother and Father gave me a fine set of watercolors for Christmas. I was proud of the set and tried very hard with painting but don't think I have a gift for it.

The Shakers speak often of gifts. If a Shaker has a special gift, then it is encouraged. The person with the gift, they say, is only the channel for the good to flow through and benefit us all. Brother Delmer has a gift for mechanical things. He built his own bench saw when he was eighteen, and the steam-fitted greenhouse only two years later. Of course he tends the Selden automobile, and he has set up a motor-driven apple grader that makes the packaging of the apples so much easier. He has so many gifts, I think he should divide them up and let others have some!

"*'Tis a gift to be simple, 'tis a gift to be free*" says one of the favorite Shaker songs.

I am not simple, nor free. I am all tangled up in worry for my brother, and I have done something I shouldn't. I suppose I will have to confess this. But I have asked Ida to ask the delivery boy — because I know she finds ways to talk to him, even though the sisters try to keep her from it — if he knows where Daniel is. She said she would. So I am waiting for the answer. And while I wait, I am looking out at the snow flying, the blur of white, and feeling the icy air, and wondering if my brother has a warm coat. And mittens. I hope he has mittens. If I had been more patient and industrious with my knitting, perhaps by now I could have made him some.

Thursday, December 12, 1918

Well! Now I have something to confess! But I think it might make Sister Jennie laugh, when the time comes.

Last evening I was working once again, after supper, on my washcloth. The other girls were all raveling haircloth and they will show me how soon so that I will be doing it, too, for the horsehair brushes are an important way to earn money for the village. But first, Sister Jennie had explained, I must master my knitting — and my impatience with it!

So last evening I was once again carefully making stitch after stitch, trying not to twist them, trying not to drop them, and, for a change, trying not to hide my mistakes but to correct them. I worked steadily along. Sister Jennie was reading aloud as we worked. She has finished *The Secret Garden* and now is reading us a book called *Toby Tyler, or Ten Weeks with a Circus* about a boy who, like some of us, is an orphan. (Isn't it odd, that so many books have orphans? Like Mary Lennox, and now Toby Tyler? And there are others, too: a boy named Freckles in a book with that title; and Pollyanna, too.) Toby is ten, and he runs away and joins a traveling circus but it is a cruel situation.

All of us love Toby and hope for the best for him. He has a pet! A chimpanzee named Mr. Stubbs! We children are not allowed pets here, although Elder William actually has a dog he calls Pup. Mother Ann's teachings are against pets, especially dogs. She taught that they are unclean and full of evil spirits! That makes me sad because a dog, or perhaps a kitten, would be a lovely thing to have, I think. And I suspect Sister Jennie thinks so, too, but of course she abides by the teachings.

Some of the girls help with gathering eggs and feeding the chickens, and they name the chickens and think of them as pets. But they aren't, really. They're ill tempered and even frightening when they flutter and peck at you. Susannah has a fierce scratch on her wrist from a chicken.

But a chimpanzee! Imagine that! We are all a bit in love with Mr. Stubbs and, of course, with Toby.

"Does a circus ever come to Sabbathday Lake?" Rebecca asked. But Sister Jennie shook her head no.

"Sometimes the circus comes to Portland," I told them. "My parents took me when I was eight and my brother was eleven. It was the only time I have ever seen an elephant."

"Were you frightened?" Grace asked.

"Not of the elephant. I just kept thinking of the Elephant's Child in *Just So Stories*. Do we have that book, Sister Jennie? I had it at home, but I don't know where it is now."

"Yea, I believe we do have a copy," she said. "We might read that one next. But let's get on now, with Toby's adventures. How's that washcloth coming, Lydia?"

When she asked me, I looked down at the needles in my hands. I realized I had been knitting the whole while, not even noticing that I was.

My fingers had been moving automatically. Into the stitch, yarn around, pull through, slip over. I knew it by heart. And now, when I looked down, I could see that a row was finished, with no mistakes, the final row on top of all those others that had been redone again and again. I held it up. A perfect square of pink yarn.

"She's finished!" Grace exclaimed. "Look, Sister Jennie! Lydia's finally finished!"

Sister Jennie set the book aside and looked. She examined it carefully, front and back, looking for my usual mistakes. Then she smiled at me. "At last!" she said. "I'll show you how to cast it off, now."

"Now you can ravel haircloth with us!" Rebecca said. The other girls groaned. Raveling haircloth wasn't fun. But at least we would be doing it together, and to make the brushes, which brought in money.

"Perhaps Lydia would like to make another washcloth," Sister Jennie said, her eyes twinkling.

"Nay," I groaned. "Never again!"

That night, when I was getting into my

nightclothes, I decided that I finally had something to confess. I would confess to her, would open my mind to her, and tell her that I had felt a great bursting of pride when I finished the silly little washcloth. Such a small thing, but it had taken me so long and I had worked so hard at it. I was very proud.

Yet Shakers, I know by now, are not supposed to feel pride. Every act of a Shaker is directed to perfection, to making a heaven on this earth. Sweeping the floor, peeling a potato, folding a pillowcase, knitting a little square. We do it perfectly. We don't take pride in that.

So I would confess to Sister Jennie about my worldly emotion.

After kneeling for prayers, the other girls and I got into our beds. Grace whispered to me, "You said 'nay' tonight."

"I did?"

Grace giggled. "About making another washcloth. It's the first time I ever heard you say it. Usually you say 'no.'"

"It was just an accident," I whispered back.

"Nay," Grace said. "It was you, becoming a Shaker."

Saturday, December 14, 1918

Some of the sisters have taken fancywork to the Poland Spring House, which is a lovely hotel, along with the Mansion House, nearby. Brother Delmer drove them there in the Selden (it would be a short buggy ride, just four miles, but the weather is very cold) and they will display the handmade goods. There are many knitted sweaters, pincushions, fans made with turkey feathers, wooden sewing carriers with handles, and poplar keepsake boxes. The other girls have been weaving the poplar cloth and I am to learn soon. The guests at the hotel often buy the Shaker fancy goods, and of course Christmas season is a busy time for sales.

One thing that the sisters will take orders for is what my father would have called a "top seller." It is an opera cloak, though now they sometimes call them "Dorothy Cloaks" after Eldress Dorothy, who first designed them. They are made in beautiful French wool lined with silk, and have a hood and a silk ribbon tie, and they cost $30! President Grover Cleveland's wife, Frances, wore one to his inauguration. But hers was gray. My favorite is a wonderful shade of red. Perhaps they will take many orders for red cloaks, this being Christmas season, and with the war over, people are wanting to celebrate.

I hope so, for these are hard times for the Shakers. I hear the sisters talking about it in worried voices. There were once so many of them! But now their numbers grow fewer and fewer, as the elders enter their spirit life, and younger sisters and brethren sometimes leave the order to join the world. The Shaker villages are getting smaller, and some, in other places, have closed. I see that they are concerned here at Sabbathday Lake about how they will survive, and about money, though at the same time they have faith that the Lord will provide, and some even predict a rebirth and many new members.

But that has not happened yet, and so they continue — I should say *we* continue — to work hard, to make new goods, to sell as much as we can, to provide for the community. At the hotel they will also sell dried herbs and candies. The candy-making shop above the laundry is filled with the smell of caramel cooking.

I am still in the kitchen, though, peeling and mashing potatoes, washing dishes, setting the tables. Sometimes I help Sister Agnes make butter. The barrel-shaped churn actually has a small motor, which makes it easier. After the butter is formed and the buttermilk is drained into pails, Sister Agnes kneads the butter with her strong hands until no more liquid comes out. Then she kneads in a little salt.

I offered to help with the kneading, but Sister Agnes laughed and said my hands are too small. But I help to shape the deep yellow rolls of butter. We put them on plates and I take them into the cold shed. In summer the shed is filled with ice that the brethren chop from the lake when the ice is thick and clear, as it is now.

But in winter there is no need for ice. The butter stays cold enough in the shed. When we need it in the kitchen, for pie crust or mashed potatoes, or just to put on bread in the dining room, we simply slice some from the roll.

There are so many different things to learn! The one I yearn to learn next is the candy-making, but by the time I get to candy-making I may be too old to have teeth! (Some of the older sisters have false ones!)

Ida knows nothing yet. But she hopes to have information soon about Daniel. She pretends that everything is very mysterious and suspenseful. I suspect she is slipping out to meet the delivery boy. But I don't want to know.

Sunday, December 15, 1918

Oh, the blessings rich and many,
Which are mine to share today!
All the fountains of God's goodness
Seem to open in my way,
Blessed fruits of sweet repentance,
Grown while stricken 'neath the rod!
Blessed lessons of instruction
Sent to lead me home to God!

That was a song sung in meeting this morning. We have sung it before and though I like the part about blessings and God's goodness, I do not care at all for the part about "stricken 'neath the rod" because I think it means that people who do wrong should be beaten. I have never seen anyone beaten here, or struck in any way, even lightly. The worst I have behaved ever was the night I shouted at Sister Jennie and said hateful things to her. Maybe I should have been stricken 'neath the rod! But she simply sent me to the retiring room to think.

Father did whip Daniel on occasion. Not with a rod, but with his belt. So did Uncle Henry. But according to the Shaker song, being stricken should make one grow into repentance. And Daniel never grew that way at all. He just grew angrier and angrier.

Oh, I do wonder and worry about my brother! Ida is no longer working in the kitchen and so she cannot see the delivery boy and will not be able to ask. I think they moved her to the laundry for that reason, so that she would stop lingering and laughing with the boy and coming back in with her cheeks all flushed.

I might try to ask the farm boy from the world who attends our school, if I can find a way. But it seems impossible. All the boys are on the other side of the classroom, beyond the big stove. We girls are not to look at them or they at us, and certainly not to talk. Daniel's desk is now empty on his side, though the boy who shared it is still there. I know Daniel talked a lot with that boy during recess. I saw them sometimes through the window.

Sister Jennie did laugh, a bit, when I confessed to her yesterday of my pride.

"Pride is a foolish thing, isn't it?" she said with a chuckle.

And I had to agree with her. Why ever did I feel so important about a silly washcloth? Making a perfect washcloth is not something to be proud about, but simply the right way—the Shaker way—to do it.

Sister Jennie read to me from Mother Ann's teachings. "'Take good care of what you have.

Provide places for your things, so that you may know where to find them, at any time, by day or by night; and learn to be neat and clean, prudent and saving, and see that nothing is lost; and be kind to the poor and needy.'"

"My house," I told her, "I mean, my house in the world? It was always neat and clean. My mother was almost like a Shaker about house-keeping!"

She smiled.

"But at Uncle Henry's! Oh, my goodness! There were things strewn everywhere. And Aunt Sarah was always blaming me, or the twins, and complaining that she couldn't find anything! I think Uncle Henry should have sent her to the Shakers!"

"It sounds to me as if she might be unhappy," Sister Jennie said.

"I never thought of that," I told her.

"Unhappiness is a kind of neediness," she pointed out.

She had just read to me about being kind to the needy, and I had thought, while she was reading: *Oh, yes, I would be very kind to needy people if I knew any.* But I wasn't at all kind to Aunt Sarah. I decided that I must think more carefully about Mother Ann's teachings and try hard to live by them.

And being kind to the poor? I think we here at Sabbathday Lake must be poor. That is why we girls work so hard on the haircloth for the brushes, and the sisters worry about the price of eggs and are so busy, always, making cloaks and candy, and the brethren make the boxes that they sell. Poor people cannot rest or waste time; they must work, always.

But I don't think we are needy. It is not the same as poor.

I am almost at the last page of this journal and I do not know what I will do when it is filled. I need a way to record my days and tell my thoughts. I am thankful every day that when I finally was brave enough to tell Sister Jennie about the journal, she viewed it as a kind of work, not something that must be shared, so she did not take it from me, as I feared she might.

Wednesday, December 18, 1918

Now, in the evenings, I am raveling haircloth with the other girls. We are each given a square of haircloth, the same kind of horsehair that covers the settee in the good room, and which stabs you with tiny prickers when you sit on it. Our job is to remove the woven hair from one edge, leaving bristles that will become a clothes brush after the brethren attach a handle. Last spring they made 840 brushes! Maybe they will do even better this spring. But of course we girls must do the raveling first. And it is not easy. Our fingers get stabbed again and again. Sister Jennie distracts us with her reading.

But now Toby's chimpanzee, Mr. Stubbs, has died! It is the saddest passage I have ever heard, in a book—the death of Mr. Stubbs. All of us wept. Even Sister Jennie had tears in her eyes. She let us set our raveling aside and we had some hot chocolate in order to recover our spirits.

Friday, December 20, 1918

Sister Mamie Curtis just got false front teeth! She smiles and smiles at everyone, to show them off.

Sunday, December 22, 1918

> *Courage! My brothers, each step bears you on,*
> *On to that beautiful home;*
> *March ye in triumph with victory crowned,*
> *Home to a heavenly home.*

Ida is gone. She ran off in the night. Maybe with the delivery boy! We girls are not supposed to know, but I could hear the sisters whispering about it in the kitchen. And there was a prayer for her at worship this morning. The prayer did not use her name, but I could tell it was about her because it mentioned sins of the flesh, and ingratitude — and forgiveness, of course.

Ida had not yet signed the covenant so she was not a true Shaker, but she had been here at Chosen Land a long time and the sisters had had hopes for her.

It was a special worship service at meeting because it is Fast Day, in preparation for Christmas. Everyone feels very solemn, and there is less food and no laughter today.

Also, on Fast Day, the Shaker covenant is read during the service—just to remind everyone, I guess, of what we are part of. It was quite long, and I'm afraid not very interesting to listen to.

I confessed that thought to Sister Jennie. Confession—opening one's mind—is also part of Christmas preparation. And I confessed something else to her, too: that Ida's leaving makes me worry a bit because it means one more person who will not be a Shaker.

Once there were thousands of Shakers, but no longer. The communities grow smaller and smaller. There are many more sisters than brethren, even here at Sabbathday Lake. I look around at my group of girls, and at the older girls who have moved to the large dwelling, and I wonder who will stay. One day I saw the two little sisters, Lillian and Pearl, playing wedding, using a torn tea towel from the mending basket as a bride's veil. I took it away from them and turned their attention elsewhere because I knew Sister Jennie would disapprove. Grace says very boldly that she wants to marry and have babies. I heard her ask Sister Jennie if she had ever wanted to have children, but Sister Jennie smiled and said, "I *do* have children. I have all of you."

Some of the sisters and brethren here are quite old and I expect that they will join the others under the stone carved with the word *Shakers* in the cemetery beside the school. Before I came, there was a brother named Eben. I heard the sisters speak about him, saying that Brother Eben had stepped out a few months ago, and at first, when they said it, I thought that he had simply walked away. But finally they explained. He had been ill, had been in the hospital for a while, but then came back to Sabbathday Lake and been tended by the sisters until he died. His earthly body rests now in the cemetery. But the important part of him stepped out to a heavenly home, as this morning's hymn describes, or to what they call the spirit world.

Sometimes Brother Delmer fetches Dr. Sturgis in the electric, and brings him to see Eldress Lizzie, or Sister Gertrude. They are both so frail.

Brother Delmer is not old, thank goodness, because I do not know what we would do without him! He fixes everything and invents new things for what can't be fixed. He even pulls teeth when necessary! Dr. Hayden, the dentist, comes occasionally for "real" dental visits. There is a special chair in the trustees' office. But when Rebecca had a loose tooth that became infected, it was Brother Delmer who pulled it. Then Rebecca had a poultice made from Shaker herbs. She held it warm against her jaw and after a few days was feeling fine.

Brother Delmer came here with his brother when he was a young boy, after their father died. A few years later, his mother came to get them. And Delmer's brother went with her. But Delmer refused. She came back several times, the sisters say, but he was steadfast and refused to go. Finally she went away for the last time, and Delmer didn't see her or his brother, Harry, for years and years. This is his *true* family.

But the family grows smaller and smaller.

Wednesday, December 25, 1918

Last night, Christmas Eve, the older girls performed a lovely Christmas pageant that they had prepared, and afterward there were gifts under a large tree in the winter chapel. Mr. Brackett, from Portland, sent a box of oranges, a real treat. Some children had gifts that family had sent. But not everyone. There was nothing from family for me. But there were things from the sisters, little things they had made, and to my delight, a special gift from Sister Jennie: a new journal to write in! She told me that the Shakers keep a journal, that one of them writes of each day's doings. So I am not the only one.

The Christmas tree surprised me, for it seems such a worldly thing. And another surprise this morning: There was also a small decorated tree in the girls' shop, and under it new games and books for our group of girls. We opened the gifts after breakfast. There was a worship service, for Christmas is like the Sabbath, and in the afternoon we amused ourselves quietly, as we would on an ordinary Sabbath. No noisy games. But new books to read! And lovely new thimbles and pincushions for us to use when we do our embroidery (some of the girls do enjoy that, though I am not one).

I carefully wrote a title page in my new journal, designating it *The Days of Lydia Pierce, 1919, Sabbathday Lake, Maine.* I will begin the actual writing of the pages in the New Year.

Friday, December 27, 1918

An ice storm. We cannot go outdoors. And one of our pipes froze and burst. Brother Delmer came and repaired the broken pipe. I think there is nothing he cannot do!

Wednesday, January 1, 1919

The first page of my new journal! I will resolve to write neatly and not to be critical of others in my writings.

Back in my other life — my past life, my life in Portland — we always made New Year's resolutions. Silly things, usually. A year ago I resolved to be more helpful to my mother around the house. Daniel resolved to pay better attention to his schoolwork. My friend Emily Ann and I resolved that we would never have foolish arguments anymore, and would be best friends forever.

Now, twelve months later, those things seem so meaningless. And here, with the Shakers, there is no talk of New Year's resolutions. I expect that if I mentioned it to Sister Jennie, she would point out that Shakers resolve in their hearts every day to be as perfect as possible, and without flaws. No Shaker needs to make a resolution for that because it is part of daily life.

But secretly, I am resolving this: to find Daniel.

There is no school now. It will resume next Monday. I am planning to find a way to talk privately with the girl named Gloria, a girl from the world who is in grade eight. I think she is the sister of the boy who was Daniel's friend at school. She may know who to ask. Somewhere, out there in the world, someone knows where Daniel has gone.

Friday, January 3, 1919

Ten inches of snow today! We are completely buried.

It is so beautiful. The white buildings of the community gleam against the sparkling snow. The huge dwelling is the only bit of color, with its reddish-pink bricks. It stands there so solid in this fairy-tale world. Icicles dangle from the eaves, and now and then we can hear one snap loose and fall. Wind picks up bits of snow and swirls it into the air. There is a huge drift against the side of the barn.

The brethren and the boys shovel and clear. The animals are warm and fed in the barn, and we are cozy in the girls' shop. We can hear the scraping sounds as the shovels make their way to us.

Saturday, January 4, 1919

A very exciting thing happened today! A sleighing party from the Mansion House came to Sabbathday Lake and stopped for a visit. They were all dressed very elegantly and had fur lap robes to keep them warm. There were no children, though. I wish there had been children.

They came into the sisters' shop and looked around, commenting very favorably about all the fancywork. And one woman bought a beautiful purple cloak for $38! The sisters handled the business very calmly but after the hotel guests had gone, they shrieked a bit and clapped their hands together in delight. It was the most expensive thing they had ever sold! I think they will set right to work on more cloaks. Maybe more purple!

They say that Elder William will take us girls for a sleigh ride soon.

Sunday, January 5, 1919

Courage! My brothers, each step bears you on,
On to that beautiful home;
March ye in triumph with victory crowned,
Home to a heavenly home.

I know that that song is talking about heaven, and not a home with a fireplace and a rocking chair. But I like to think that "brothers stepping on to a beautiful home" is referring to Daniel, and that he will somehow step on to a place where he is happy.

Monday, January 6, 1919

School has reopened after a vacation for the holidays, and our feet crunch on the packed snow as we walk along the paths to work and to breakfast and then across the road to the schoolhouse. The snow on either side is taller than most of us.

I had made up my mind to ask the girl, Gloria, if she knew anything about my brother. She is a pleasant enough girl, blonde and freckled, though not terribly bright and I fear she may not stay in school until she graduates. I have not spoken much to her before, but today, standing near her as we warmed ourselves at the woodstove, I smiled and asked if her family had fared comfortably through the big snowstorm.

"It was hard getting here today," she said. "The road's only part plowed. My brother stayed home to help clear."

So I was right. She is the sister of Daniel's friend. I remembered that his name is Eli. His desk was empty today.

I would have said more, but the teacher called us to sit down then, and as always the school day began with the Lord's Prayer. I waited impatiently throughout the morning for another chance to talk to Gloria. Because of the deep snow we did not have outdoor recess, but when there came a time that Gloria excused herself to go to the outhouse, beside the woodshed, I waited a few moments and then got permission to go as well. I met her on the shoveled path.

"I've been wondering if you would ask your brother something for me," I told her.

She looked at me curiously. It was cold outside, and we both had our arms wrapped around ourselves for warmth. I could see that her fingernails were dirty.

"You remember Daniel? He shared Eli's desk. I think they were friends."

"Oh, sure, I remember that boy," she said. "Eli said he's very smart. Could do all the math easy. Eli has trouble with math."

"He's my brother."

She looked at me curiously, at my Shaker-made clothes. "But he went away, and you stayed?"

I nodded. "Yea. I mean *yes*. He ran off."

"You looking to find him?" She shivered in the wind. "We gotta go in. It's too cold."

I followed her to the schoolhouse. "Can you help me? Can you ask Eli?"

"Don't let the cold in, girls," Sister Cora called when we opened the door. "Hurry inside!"

Gloria and I went to our desks. At noon, when the bell rang for dinner and I went for my jacket where it hung on its peg, I passed her seat and she whispered to me, "I'll ask."

Thursday, January 9, 1919

It is so cold now, below zero, that Sister Cora will not hold school tomorrow. The children from the world cannot make their way to school in this cold, not with the wind blowing, for fear of frostbite, and the large schoolroom, though it stays warm by the stove, is very drafty around the windows. We wear scarves around our necks. Our fingers become stiff. And the ink in our ink pots is thickened by the chill.

There is a wood furnace in the girls' shop. We take turns bringing in wood from the storage place off the porch, and we stay cozy, though the retiring rooms are chilly. Brother Delmer rises very early, before anyone, and starts the fires in the stoves in the laundry and ironing rooms.

I helped make apple pies for tonight's supper. One more Shaker invention: an apple-peeling device! It makes it so much easier. While Sister Hazel rolled out the crusts on the marble slab in the baking room, I peeled apple after apple, turning the little handle that makes the device revolve against the blade. Then Grace, who was also helping, sliced them into a large bowl and added sugar and cinnamon. The cores and peelings are saved for the animals. While the pies were baking in the large brick oven, Eliza (who lives on the third floor of the girls' shop, along with her sister Lila — they will be moving soon to the big dwelling) whipped some cream that had been separated off the top of the milk and set aside. Sister Sirena prepared the fish chowder, and Grace and I got the dishes in order for the meal.

There is so much work in preparing meals three times a day, and the cleanup afterward! But we have become a sort of team, each of us knowing our role. And I do love the kitchen, with its fine smells, and the cheerful conversation among the sisters.

Outside, the wind was howling, and as the supper hour approached we could hear the brethren and boys come from their side of the dwelling, stamping snow from their feet, hanging their jackets, and moving into their silent waiting space beyond the dining room. They had been out in that bitter weather, feeding and watering the animals, milking the cows, preparing the barns for night. Their faces and hands, I knew, would be red with cold and their breath coming in short, steamy gasps. Now, in the place where they waited for the dinner bell, they sat, became quiet, and let the warmth come through them.

The sisters and girls were entering on the other side. The wind continued battering at the brick walls of the dwelling. It swept up the hillside across the road and bent the trees there. The sky was very dark and the golden gaslight from the windows reflected on the icy snowdrifts. In the barn, I suppose the oxen and other animals were snorting and shifting in their stalls. Everyone is looking for warmth.

Friday, January 10, 1919

It is four degrees below zero. No school still. Brother Delmer comes to check our pipes. He tells us to leave a little water running. That will help to keep them from freezing. Usually Sister Jennie scolds us if we leave water running! But now we follow his instructions because it is terrible when the pipes freeze and burst.

Tuesday, January 14, 1919

School has resumed but Gloria is absent. Her brother Eli is, as well. The students from the world are most likely absent, I think, because their families need their help in this cold. There is wood to be brought in, fires to tend, animals who need feeding and watering. Clothes must be dried and warmed, and even cooking is different, and harder, when farmhands need to be nourished with hot soups and stews. The same is true here, and we work hard in the kitchen to keep up the strength and the spirits of the men and boys who come in chilled to the bone.

But fortunately no one is ill, except Brother John Dorrington, who is not at all well and may be slipping toward spirit life, they say. The rest of us are red-cheeked and hearty, even those with tooth trouble, ear trouble, heart trouble.

We are fortunate. In school today, Sister Cora talked of the influenza epidemic.

I knew, of course, from my own family what a terrible toll it had taken. But I did not know how many millions of others had perished. Over 25 million — some say 50 million — all around the world! The King of Spain, and the son of the French Premier — both lost to the flu. In this country, our Assistant Secretary of the Navy was taken ill in September, when he was on a ship, and had to be carried ashore, unable to walk, and spent weeks recovering. He was a young man, and not a famous name — I didn't recognize it — Franklin Delano Roosevelt. But he survived. So many others did not. In the town of Bath, there were 3,000 cases of influenza, and three young nurses who had volunteered to help were stricken and lost their lives: Harriet Bliss, Alice Dain, and Adelaide Hogue.

Many more Americans died in the epidemic than in the war.

The Maine Department of Health has built an emergency corps of doctors and nurses so that they will be prepared if such a disaster ever strikes again. This time, there were not enough medical people to deal with the sick, and no one knows that better than me. We were alone in our house, with no doctor who could come, and though I have no way of knowing, I expect that in our pretty little Woodfords neighborhood we were not the only ones. Perhaps house after house experienced what my family did, each of us alone and afraid.

Though except for the reciting of the Lord's Prayer each morning, we do not ordinarily pray in school, today we paused and bowed our heads to remember those who had entered into spirit life, and to give thanks for our good health. Funny little Lillian Beckwith announced, midprayer, "But Pearl and me have sniffles!" and I could see Sister Cora, usually so stern, smile slightly.

They say that because women played such a valuable role in both the war and the epidemic, they may soon be given the right to vote! The U.S. Congress must pass the 19th Amendment to the Constitution, which will grant them that right.

Women and men have always been equal in the Shaker faith. It is part of Mother Ann's teachings.

I must say that I find her teachings very wise, all but the no-pets part. And I have some worries about the no-marriage. Certainly, it is true that one concentrates more on one's faith and work if one is not distracted by romance and marriage and babies.

But where will the Shakers of the future come from?

Friday, January 17, 1919

Gloria and Eli are both back in school and have brought me news of Daniel!

Eli could not speak to me, of course, because it is not allowed. But Gloria took me aside at recess while the other girls were playing stoop tag in the road beside the cemetery.

"At first Eli didn't want to tell me because he promised Daniel he wouldn't say anything," Gloria said. "But I said I'd help him with his Geography homework, and so finally he gave in and said Daniel's in Oxford Hills."

Oxford Hills! That's not very far away!

"He told Eli he was going to hitch a ride on

a train and go out west, or if he didn't do that maybe he could go on a fishing boat. They hire young boys."

I shuddered. Winter on a fishing boat off the coast of Maine! I couldn't imagine Daniel out there on the sea, freezing and wet and probably scared.

Gloria giggled. "He should join a circus!"

I didn't think that was funny. All boys say they're going to run off to a circus, but I know from hearing Sister Jennie read *Toby Tyler* that no good comes of that dream!

"Anyway," she went on, "he only got as far as Oxford Hills. He didn't have any money, and he tried to talk Mr. Melby at the general store into giving him some food for free, if he swept the floor and straightened the shelves. Mr. Melby felt sorry for him and took him on as a helper. He sleeps on the floor in the storeroom."

"On the floor? But here in the boys' shop he had a warm bed! And three good meals every day!"

Gloria shrugged.

"And what about school?" I was almost wailing. "Our parents thought school was so important! And Daniel is *smart*!"

"I expect he has to do some arithmetic there in the store," Gloria said. I could see she was trying to make me feel better. "The storekeeper has to add up what people spend. And make change."

I groaned. Our father had worked in a store. He added things up and made change. He smiled at customers and was polite to them when they complained. But in the evenings, at supper, he told us how our lives would be better than his. He said Daniel would go to college and become a lawyer. He had the knack for arguing, Father said, and would be a good one.

The bell rang for the end of recess. I followed Gloria back toward the schoolhouse. "Daniel liked the animals," I said in despair. "He knows them as if they were people. He said there was one heifer . . ."

"Well, Mr. Melby has a cat, I think," Gloria said cheerfully. "I suppose Daniel can put its food down for it, and clean the dish."

Clean the cat's dish! Poor Daniel! I wanted to weep.

Monday, January 20, 1919

We girls were given the news this morning that Elder William Dumont would be taking us on a sleigh ride after school! What excitement! We could hardly concentrate on our studies, and at noon, at dinner, it was hard to be silent. We glanced at each other and occasionally whispered and giggled. Sister Jennie said that if we didn't behave, she would go and sit at another table, so we tried to contain ourselves. But surely it was the most exciting occasion in a very long time, maybe even better than Christmas.

Finally Sister Cora dismissed us early from school and we ran to the girls' shop to change our clothes and bundle ourselves for our outing. After a bit, Elder William drove the horses — their sleigh bells making wonderful music — and sleigh up to the end of our path and we all went out and climbed aboard. There were thick blankets over our laps.

I was a little nervous about being with Elder William. He and Eldress Lizzie Noyes are the most important people in our community, and he of course is a man, which makes me shy around him.

It was Elder William who created the water tower here at Sabbathday Lake. He did it after so much of the Shaker community in Alfred was destroyed by fire. Fortunately no one died in that fire, but their buildings burned, and Elder William determined that it should not happen here. So the water tower was built on top of the hill, and designed with waterworks that spray water all over our buildings. Elder William has tested the system and they say it throws water all the way up to the cupola on the big brick dwelling.

There was a time when he was in charge of the farming, and he also supervised the construction of the big brick dwelling with its 48 rooms in 1884. Here is a passage in the daily journal that is kept so carefully: "July 19, 1887: Elder William got up at 2 o'clock this morning. Goes to the Stable, feeds the horses, builds fires at the Wash House. Starts the mowing machines at 3:30, mowed 'til 6 o'clock then starts off to the Depot with Elder John. A hard morning's work to do before breakfast."

Sister Cora let us read some older entries in the Shaker journal because she wanted us to see, and to copy, the beautiful penmanship. One Shaker is assigned the job of "scribe" and writes the entries with a pen. I don't believe I will ever become scribe. My writing is messy, with ink blots, though I try hard.

The entry I copied, about Elder William, was written 32 years ago. We are not allowed to see newer entries. I suspect there must be one dated last October 22nd, which says something like, "A new girl was brought to us today. She wore a very dirty dress and was rude to Sister Jennie, but we hope that with guidance her deportment will improve. Her name is Lydia Pierce."

Elder William is getting older now and slowing down a bit. Last year he turned over the care of the family garden to Brother Delmer. But he still leads worship, prepares supplies for the sisters' fancywork, and is a mentor and caretaker of the boys. He must be saddened by my brother's leave-taking, I think, and I decided that even if we entered into conversation during the sleigh ride, I would not mention Daniel.

I did wonder if perhaps he would drive the horses past the general store in Oxford Hills and if I might catch a glimpse of my brother. But instead he turned the horses toward Poland Spring and to the Mansion House, four miles distant. The horses were familiar with the road, it was clear. They trotted with their feet high, heads bobbing, and their harness bells ringing. The cold air reddened our cheeks. We sped along on the packed snow and we girls sang one Shaker song after another. To my surprise, Elder William joined in with a rousing, deep voice. I have heard him sing with the others at worship but this was different—this was singing for pure fun.

We were breathless with singing and laughing when we reached the hotel and Elder William pulled the horses to a stop. He lifted us down one by one and we were invited inside! The hotel owners, the Rickers, are very good friends of the

Shakers. In fact, they come to our worship service many Sundays. So we were greeted warmly and given delicious hot chocolate to drink while we stood in the lobby, awed by the furniture and carpets and draperies — so different from our plain, scrubbed life.

It was already dark when we got back, and the other girls and I were late for our kitchen work, but the sisters had done our chores for us and were glad that we had had such an excursion. Perhaps all of them have been on sleigh rides from time to time.

Friday, January 24, 1919

The brethren are cutting ice today, from the lake. It is good clear ice, twelve inches thick. The ice house is almost full.

Saturday, January 25, 1919

Brother John Dorrington has passed into the spirit world. He was a devoted worker in the community and will be greatly missed.

Sunday, February 2, 1919

Let my name be recorded
In the book the angels keep
Where each act is rewarded
And the seed I have sown I shall reap.
So when the angel reaper cometh,
And the harvest time shall be,
I shall find in my Father's house,
There's a mansion reserved for me.

I know, I know, once again the song is talking about passing into the spirit life (we prayed for Brother John Dorrington at worship last Sunday). But all I can think about when we sing "there's a mansion reserved for me" is the Mansion House at Poland Spring, where just two weeks ago I stood in all that splendor and sipped hot chocolate.

On occasion Elder William or Brother Delmer drives some sisters to the Mansion House to set up a sale of fancy goods in the lobby. I hope one day I will be allowed to go and help. The wealthy guests all buy our goods enthusiastically and comment on the fine quality of the work. (The sisters do not include my terrible knitting in the sale!)

One of our biggest sellers is our poplar boxes. And now (though I had hoped my next stint would be candy-making!) I am learning to weave poplar.

I miss the kitchen. But all of our work is important to the community, so I am trying hard to do a good job of weaving. All of the girls except the smallest ones must learn, and then we must each turn out six inches or more a day in winter, to keep the supply of poplar cloth adequate for the many, many boxes. Each one requires a great deal of work. The hardest part of the job is for the brethren and boys, for they are the ones who must cut down the poplar trees, freeze the wood, and then cut it into thin, thin strips, a number of them held together at the top by an uncut section. Then the strips are to be woven.

The looms are in the sisters' shop, near the laundry, in the weaving room. Two girls sit side by side on stools at huge wooden looms, and weave together. We work the pedals with our feet, separating the warp thread that Sister Mamie has already set for us. Then, carefully, we take one thin strip of damp poplar — it is waiting, rolled in a wet towel, because if it is dry it will snap and break — hold it by wooden tongs, and work it through, then bring the batten down against it to tighten it, then use the foot pedal again, throw a wooden bobbin, and bring the batten against it one more time. We do this again and again until we have woven our six inches. If we don't finish before school, we must go back after.

I am sitting beside Lila McCool, Eliza's sister, to work. She is faster than I am because she has been doing it longer. But she is patient and waits for me to get it right.

The poplar cloth is used for the boxes, which are made in all sizes. Satin or velvet lines the heavy cardboard frame, and then the poplar cloth is wired to it on the outside, with fine wire. We cover the wires with kidskin, and then use ribbon to attach the lid in a pretty way, and to decorate the elastic, which goes around a button to make a catch.

Many sisters work on these, and sometimes Elder William loads the buggy with such wares and travels great distances to sell them. The most elegant ladies use the poplar boxes to hold their sewing, and if they ever chance to turn their sewing box upside down, they will see "USS Sabbathday Lake, Me." stamped on the bottom. *USS* means "United Society of Shakers." I suggested to Sister Mamie that we could add our own initials in a corner—very small—so if a society lady saw, for example, "LAP" in pretty penmanship, she would know that Lydia Amelia Pierce had decorated her poplar box. But Sister Mamie was shocked at the thought. She reminded me that Shakers never seek admiration for our work, only the approval of the Lord for our industriousness.

Well, she seeks admiration for her new false teeth! She displays them all the time, she is so proud. But of course I did not say that to her.

There is rarely a moment of the day when we—the sisters, and the girls—are not working: sewing, knitting, raveling, weaving, cleaning, cooking, packaging herbs, or attending school or Sunday School or worship services. We are always, always busy! I barely have time to write in this journal, but Sister Jennie sometimes allows me to go early to the retiring room for that purpose.

Right now it is Sunday afternoon, our time of leisure. The other girls are downstairs reading *Little Women* aloud, passing the book from girl to girl (and trying to be very patient and helpful when Pearl and Lillian struggle with the long words). I have read it before, many times, and in the past, thinking about the March family, I always wished I had a house full of sisters. Now I feel as if I do. Grace would be Beth, I think, so sweet and dear. Polly, studious and spectacled, would be Meg. We don't, at Sabbathday Lake, have anyone like Amy, so vain! But I will put Rebecca in that role, because she is artistic, like Amy. And me — of course I am Jo.

Wednesday, February 12, 1919

Finally, finally, today was a day when all of the girls who are weaving poplar had finished the required amount before school. Polly, who has an ironing stint now, had done all of her handkerchiefs, and for the first time in a long while we had time to play after school. All of us girls from the girls' shop! Sister Jennie shooed us outdoors for exercise because our energy, she said, was becoming noisy in the house.

The younger girls, like Pearl and Lillian, who don't have to weave, have been working on building a snow cave behind the girls' shop, near the lilacs, which form a playhouse in summer. But the snow is thick and heavy. It is hard work for them, and they were glad when we bigger girls offered to help.

We dug and piled and scooped and carved and shaped. At first we called it our fort. But Sister Ada happened by on her way to the sisters' shop, where she works on candy-making. Sister Ada is a gentle soul, mild-mannered and quiet. But when she asked about our structure and Lillian called out, "It's a fort!" I could see the look on her face. She was quite shocked. So I corrected Lillian and said, "Nay, it's an igloo! We've been learning in school about Eskimos!" Sister Ada smiled then, and nodded in approval.

When she had gone on, I whispered to the

other girls, "*Fort* is what the army has. We mustn't build a fort!"

"Why not?" asked Lillian, as she smoothed snow on the rounded side of the igloo.

"It's military," Polly explained. "Don't you pay attention in Sunday School? We're pacifists. We can't even play at war.

"It's Mother Ann's teachings," she added.

"Oh," Lillian said matter-of-factly. "Yea. I forgot. Well, I like Eskimos. Look! The door to the igloo's ready!"

We took turns going inside. Three people could fit at a time, so three would be Eskimo wives, cooking blubber in the igloo, and the others were the hunters and fishermen, out roaming the yard, looking for prey. Polly dragged back a piece of wood and called it a seal.

The light was pale blue inside. When it was my turn, I crawled in after Grace, and after me came Rebecca. We crouched on the snow in a circle.

"We are the three wives of Ukluk!" Grace intoned. "He has gone to capture a whale!"

Rebecca collapsed in giggles. "Three wives!"

"Yea," Grace whispered, "and we will bear him many babies! I'm going to have one very soon!" With her mittened hands she pushed the front of her thick jacket forward to make a round belly. "It will be a son and I will name him 'Owa Tagoo Siam.' Say it after me."

Rebecca and I chanted the words. "Owa Tagoo Siam . . ."

"Faster!" Grace ordered. "Louder!"

"Owa Tagoo Siam! OWA TAGOO SIAM!"

Grace shrieked with laughter and finally we realized what we were saying—*Oh, what a goose I am!*—and collapsed in giggles.

Elvira's head appeared in the doorway to the igloo. "Our turn now!" she said loudly.

We stopped laughing and scrambled out of the igloo to give the other girls a turn.

In the waiting room before supper, where we are always supposed to be so quiet and to prepare ourselves for the meal, we glanced at each other and formed the words silently with our mouths: *owa tagoo.* . . . Then we had to bite our lips to keep from laughing aloud.

When the bell finally rang for us to enter the dining room, Sister Jennie rearranged our seating so that the three of us, Rebecca, Grace, and me, would not be together. When we knelt, I said the usual prayer silently: "I pray God bless me, and give me grace, and make me a good child."

Then I was able to turn my attention away from the foolishness. I felt my face become solemn and calm. Sister Jennie looked at me understandingly and smiled. I somehow think that there was a time in her life when she, too, was a silly young girl.

Sunday, February 16, 1919

Give me a name that all can bless,
A name that God can love;
One that will brightly shine on earth,
And brighter glow above.

I sort the little stones that I keep now in the box that Daniel made for me. My little family. It has grown larger, actually. First Grace begged me to add her little purple stone, and then when I showed the collection to the other girls, they all went and found stones as well. There is a place by the corner of the barn where the snow blows away and leaves the ground exposed. They found stones there, and so now I have two small ones that are Lillian and Pearl, and larger ones for Eliza, Lila, Rebecca, and Polly. Names that God can love, as this morning's song said.

I wonder if an Eskimo really could be named Ukluk, and whether God loves that name as well. Sister Jennie would say yes.

But Sister Jennie would also hope that Ukluk would become a Shaker!

Gloria, at school (I think I will add a stone for her as well), tells me that she has seen Daniel. He was unloading a wagon that had brought goods to the Oxford Hills store. Gloria was there with her mother to buy lamp oil and sugar. Mr. Melby at the store sold them those things, and she could see Daniel at work in back, lifting the crates.

"How did he look?" I asked.

Gloria shrugged. "He looked all right."

I meant *Did he look happy? Did he look healthy?* But Gloria is a very simple girl. I don't think she would be able to say those things. So I had to settle for "He looked all right."

Yesterday I went to Sister Jennie for confession, to open my mind to her. I have such small things to confess. I did not finish my full six inches of poplar cloth weaving on Tuesday (but I made up for it the next day). Grace and Polly and I were mean to Rebecca and went off without her instead of waiting after school one afternoon, and her feelings were hurt.

We talked about responsibility and kindness.

I have not confessed to Sister Jennie that Gloria tells me about Daniel. I don't think it is sinful, worrying about my brother. But having secrets, I know, is not a good thing. Secrets gnaw at your insides. If I feel the gnawing, I will talk about it to Sister Jennie. But not yet.

I did tell her one thing that troubles me greatly — that I cannot really remember my baby sister. I can no longer see Lucy's face or smell the sweet powdery smell of her after Mother gave her a bath. All of that seems to have drifted away.

We talked about spirits, and the spirit world. Sister Jennie told me that Lucy lives on there. Sometimes one can even see spirits! Sister Jennie never has. But she told me that after Brother Eben entered the spirit life—not long after—one of the sisters saw him standing in a doorway. Then he drifted away, through a wall. And some years ago, when Elder John Vance was very ill in the Alfred community, his spirit was seen on the stairs here at Chosen Land. Later, word came that he had passed on.

"Is it frightening, do you think?" I asked her. "To see a spirit?"

She laughed. "Oh, nay. They are part of us."

So if I can't remember Lucy's face or her sweet smell, it doesn't matter. She is part of me for always.

Thursday, February 20, 1919

This afternoon, after school, I was sent to help with the making of applesauce. Although many sisters help, Eldress Lizzie Noyes is the one who is in charge of applesauce, which is made using the dried apples combined with cider. Applesauce is another way of making money for the community. Usually Eldress Lizzie and her helpers make 50 gallons at a time. Being there, helping, reminded me of the many times I helped in the kitchen with pies: the wonderful smell of apples and cinnamon.

I confess, though, I did not really help very much. Eldress Lizzie was suffering from a severe earache. So she was seated in a rocker, supervising, and I went and sat beside her to keep her company. The other sisters suggested it. She and I talked quietly together.

Eldress Lizzie told me that her mother's name was Lydia, like me! After her mother died, her father and uncle became Shakers, and she came to the community with them. She was 16. But she did not stay, when she was grown. She went away to school and became a teacher out in the world. She taught school in Missouri for a time, but after a visit back to Sabbathday Lake, she decided to join the community. She returned to Missouri one more time, and then came back and "put on the Shaker dress," as she described. She was almost 30 when she signed the covenant, along with Mary Grant, Sirena Douglas, Sarah Fletcher, and Amanda Stickney. She has been here ever since.

When she came, she told me, there were 68 Shakers at Sabbathday Lake. Now there are many fewer. But Eldress Lizzie believes that there will be a new spurt of growth in the Shaker population. Mother Ann prophesied that the numbers would grow small but then there would be a resurgence of believers. Eldress Lizzie and Elder William Dumont (they govern the community jointly, for Mother Ann's teachings declare equality of the sexes in all departments) pray for that resurgence every day.

Her health is a little frail now that she is elderly. With her heart problems, she no longer drives the horses.

It was Eldress Lizzie who arranged for the community to have a telephone, and also — imagine this! — she was the one who bought the automobile, the Selden, ten years ago!

She did not complain about the pain in her ears, and she seemed to enjoy our conversation. But Sister Elizabeth whispered to me that I should be as quiet as possible because Eldress Lizzie was suffering. She will be taken to the doctor in Portland as soon as possible.

Walking back to the girls' shop to tidy myself before supper, I stopped by the sheltered place where there is no snow and we can still find stones. It was cold and getting dark, but I leaned down and looked carefully and found a white one. Then, back in my room, I added Eldress Lizzie to my stone family. Her hair, beneath her Shaker cap, is white.

Saturday, February 22, 1919

Some of the sisters took newly made candy to the Mansion House to sell. They have been working on the candy for the past several days. Rebecca is working on the candy-making now, and I suppose when I open my mind to Sister Jennie next, I will have to confess to jealousy. I *so* want to work on the candy! But instead I am making applesauce and weaving poplar cloth, and washing pots and pans. Next I will be helping to package herbs. Do they not *see* that I would be very, very good at candy-making?

Thursday, February 27, 1919

The Shakers don't celebrate their "real" birthdays, but instead what they call their "came among believers" day — the day that they entered the Shaker community. For me and my brother that would be October 22nd, the day we arrived at Sabbathday Lake.

But today — February 27th — is Daniel's real fifteenth birthday.

He was three when I was born. Mother said that he could not pronounce my name, and he called me Lyddie. He mixed it up with the word *little*, and he referred to me as "the lyddie baby" and made everyone laugh.

His own name is Daniel Walter Pierce, named for his father and grandfather. Never once was he called Dan or Danny.

He taught me to throw a ball and to say the

Pledge of Allegiance. We say it now each day in the Shaker school, and when I begin the words "I pledge allegiance to my flag . . ." I always remember Daniel showing me how to hold my hand over my heart.

He is no more than eight miles away from me now, but the distance seems a great one and impossible to bridge. I hope he thinks of me, of his Lyddie, and I pray that I will see him again in this life.

Sunday, March 2, 1919

With a new tongue I now will speak
And keep the valley lowly
I'll watch my thoughts and words this week
And have them pure and holy

Sister Helen moved her hands in a particular way with this song, and the other sisters and the brethren joined in. It is called "motioning" and is not at all the same as the whirling and dancing and marching that Shakers once did. We girls watched and tried to do the same motions with our hands.

If we were doing this as a game, we would laugh at our own mistakes. But we do not laugh during the Sabbath meeting. Everything is quite solemn.

It is March. I have been here for four months. And still they have not set me to candy-making. It is hard to keep my thoughts pure and holy when I think about that.

Tuesday, March 11, 1919

Eldress Lizzie has been in Portland for several days, having her ears tended to by doctors. It seems strange without her here to lead us into the dining room, and to indicate when the meal has ended. Eldress Prudence takes her place — she is the "Second Eldress" and is in charge of the younger sisters and also those girls who have moved over to the dwelling, as I will when I turn thirteen.

The brethren are working very hard at the moment on brush-making. They make 70 a day, using the raveled horsehair that we girls have prepared. When they finish, they will have almost a thousand brushes to sell. And in the sisters' shop, they are working on cloaks. We need the money for taxes.

(Of course if they had more candy-makers, it would be a help, I think.)

Gloria has no more news for me of Daniel. His desk, beside Eli, is still empty, and when I ask Gloria, she simply shrugs. At recess she spends her time with the other girls from the world, Louise and Marian. They ignore the Shaker girls like me.

Thursday, March 13, 1919

Brother Delmer went to Portland in the automobile and brought Eldress Lizzie back to Sabbathday Lake. She is feeling very cheerful with her ears no longer aching, and we are glad to have her back with us.

The boys have a sled that they are allowed to use when they have recreation time. They come flying down the hill behind the schoolhouse, shouting and laughing. We can see, and even *hear*, them from the windows of the girls' shop.

I pointed out to Sister Jennie that Mother Ann said males and females are equal — it is an important part of the teachings — and so we girls should have a turn with the sled.

She is thinking about that, and she may ask Eldress Lizzie to discuss it with Elder William. I think he will agree, because it was he who took the girls on a sleigh ride and so he has seen how much we enjoy being out in the cold, fresh air. And we do not shout as the boys do.

I think Daniel would enjoy the sledding.

It is almost spring, but in Maine the date of spring doesn't mean much. It is still cold, and there is still a great deal of snow on the ground. On March 30th we will start Daylight Savings Time and it will be light at suppertime.

Monday, March 17, 1919

It is not that I am too young for candy-making. Susannah has been doing it, and she is just my age! She lives in the girls' shop and sleeps in the retiring room across the hall, with Elvira Brooks and the Holt sisters. Ordinarily I like Susannah. But lately she has been commenting too often about what hard work it is, making taffy and caramels.

And not only that, but Elvira and Polly are both starting piano lessons! They go, one at a time, to practice in the good room while the others of us have to listen to them from the room where we are doing our endless knitting. Their piano playing is just as bad as my knitting, maybe worse!

I would like piano lessons! And I would like to make candy! Instead, Sister Jennie is teaching me to sew so that I can make my own dresses as all the older girls do. I hate sewing and I hate knitting and I hate ironing and . . .

Oh, hating is a terrible sin, I know. So is envy. One of the seven deadlies. But still!

Saturday, March 22, 1919

I opened my mind to Sister Jennie today and told her about all the hating and envying I had been feeling. I thought she would lecture me and I thought that I deserved the lecture.

She did, at first, remind me of one of Mother Ann's teachings, one we girls had learned in

Sunday School: "Labor to make the way of God your own. Let it be your inheritance, your treasure, your occupation, your daily calling."

I promised I would try.

And then, instead of a lecture, she taught me a new song! We sang it together. To be honest, Sister Jennie does not have a very pretty singing voice, not like the four sisters over at the Canterbury Shaker community in New Hampshire who have made a quartet and take the Shaker songs out to the world.

But Sister Jennie and I sang together . . .

> *I will bow and be simple*
> *I will bow and be free*
> *I will bow and be humble*
> *Yea bow like the willow tree*

. . . and I realized that the lecture I deserved was in the song itself.

I must learn to bow.

Tuesday, April 1, 1919

We girls sat in the wrong desks at school today, and then said "April Fool!" when Sister Cora looked askance at us. She didn't laugh, just directed us sternly to our assigned seats.

In the afternoon, Eliza used the telephone at the girls' shop (Sister Jennie was busy elsewhere and didn't know) to call the trustees' office and tell Brother Delmer that our pipes were frozen. He was quite surprised because the weather has been warming and the snow is even beginning to melt a bit. But he came immediately with his tools. And he *did* laugh when we all cried, "April Fool!"

After supper, back at the girls' shop, we had one more joke to play. Susannah had secretly brought candy wrappers from the candy-making room in the sisters' shop, where she had been working. She and I carefully wrapped the stones that I had saved for such a long time, the ones I pretended were my family. I saved only one, the little pink one that I called Lucy for my baby sister. The others didn't seem important keepsakes anymore. There were so many of them, because I had added stones for each of the sisters and the girls as well. My family had become very large! And now we wrapped them each in a candy wrapper, and after supper we announced we had a surprise, and passed them around as all the girls and Sister Jennie settled into their chairs to start the evening of fancywork and story reading.

Of course they discovered the trick very quickly. We announced "April Fool!" and gathered up the stones. Sister Jennie shook her head at our foolishness.

Then she opened her book and began to read aloud. But it was *The Five Little Peppers*, which we had finished such a long time ago! When she saw our faces, she said, "April Fool!" and picked up the real story.

Tuesday, April 8, 1919

Yesterday afternoon, after school, I walked up the road to the trustees' office because Dr. Hayden, the dentist, had come, and he was to examine my teeth. Sister Ada Frost was just coming out when

I got there and she was looking a little pained, so I expect she had needed a filling. (I was lucky. I didn't.)

Just as we were passing each other on the steps at the entrance, we heard a noise above. Sister Ada and I both looked up. There, in the sky, a V of geese was flying noisily past. Perhaps, Sister Ada said, they would remain at Chosen Land for the summer instead of going farther north. She said there are always waterfowl on Sabbathday Lake in summer.

I have never been here in summer. But the other girls say that we can swim and pick berries and have picnics.

Walking back to the girls' shop after my time with Dr. Hayden, I noticed that the willow trees are beginning to turn pale green. The tall oaks and maples are still stark, with bare branches against the sky. They will not have leaves for another month. The willows are always the earliest, brightening that way when there is still snow on the ground, reminding us that spring is coming, that the earth is renewing itself.

At home, at my first home, in the world,

Mother always brought in bare forsythia branches and placed them in water so that they would burst into their yellow bloom for Easter. She called it "forcing"—making them bloom early.

No one is forcing the willows. They are eager. For the first time I noticed how they do curve and bow gracefully, their pale green looping down toward the piled snow.

Saturday, April 12, 1919

Yesterday afternoon we could hear the boys shouting, "Ice out! Ice out!" Everyone in Maine knows what that means. The thick ice coating the lake is beginning to crack and break. Wide holes are opening and you can see the dark, cold water. From here we could hear the sound last night as the ice chunks moved and ground against each other.

The snow has melted so much that the top of the high grass is exposed. The sky is blue today, with high, thin clouds here and there.

This morning, as we cleaned our rooms, we girls kept going to the windows and looking out at the fields beyond the barn. The men and boys are turning the animals out. They have been cooped up in their stalls for months. Now they step out into the air, curious and excited. Some of the young cattle run, kicking their heels up. Their breath comes in steamy bursts.

Sister Jennie came in to remind us to go back to our sweeping, but then she, too, went to the window and watched. There are so many of them! They stream out, urged forward by the men and boys, who shout at them and slap their rumps. Then they move across and out. The fields go on and on. By evening, Sister Jennie says, they will come back up to the rear of the barn for hay that will be strewn for them. But now, in daytime, they explore the outdoors they have not seen for months. They nudge at the snow, pull at the old grass, run at each other as if in play.

After the cattle, the horses emerge: the two big draft horses, and the two sleeker driving horses, then the old one, the one that doesn't work anymore, that plods out and looks around. And the mules, too. They all still have their heavy winter coats but soon they will shed, rubbing themselves against the bark of trees.

We girls are not allowed to go down to the barn because that is the boys' place. But after dinner, in the afternoon, we foolishly played at being cattle and horses, galloping up and down the road, snorting and tossing our heads. The sisters, out and about at their tasks, watched us and laughed.

Wednesday, April 16, 1919

It is ten in the morning, and we are neither in school nor at work. Some of the girls are crying. All of us are very frightened. There is nothing we can do but wait, and watch, and pray, because a frightful thing has happened.

Yesterday was such a beautiful day . . . so springlike. We watched the young cattle lope out across the fields, so happy to be free of the barn. None of us had any hint of what was to come. There were clouds in the sky, and the weather grew chilly at suppertime. No one gave it a thought.

But sometime in the night, the wind came up,

and with it, snow. In mid-April! It is very rare. It began to snow and grew worse and worse, with the wind howling. It became a blizzard. By morning, when we woke, we could see nothing outside — just the whirling white. From the girls' shop (I am looking through the window now) the brick dwelling next door is not visible. There is *nothing* visible but snow.

In the past, during snowstorms, the boys delivered food to the girls' shop so that we would be warm and fed before they shoveled out the paths. But this morning they could not. Sister Jennie had a call on the telephone, very early. The men and boys have all gone out to try to find and save the animals. Can you imagine! In this blinding snow and bitterly cold wind, they have made their way, calling to one another since they can see nothing, out into the fields. Some of the men are too elderly to undertake such a dangerous job. Elder William will come here very shortly and lead us all over to the dining room and kitchen, where we will be warm and can help prepare food for those who make their way back.

We are afraid for the men and boys who are out there, blindly searching in the howling blizzard. We are afraid for the animals, who are frightened and cold and unfed.

And we are afraid for Chosen Land. If we were to lose the herd of cattle — and the horses —

I hear Elder William stamping his feet on the porch. I must hurry.

Later. 2 p.m.

I tucked my journal inside my jacket and now I have it here, in the dwelling. Sister Jennie said I might use this time to write. "Yea," she said, when I asked permission. "This is our history you are writing."

The wind has died a little, though the snow still swirls. Through a window I can see a corner of the barn. When we came this morning from the girls' shop, it was still blowing and impossible to see. Elder William led us. We all held hands and formed a line, the littlest girls in the middle and Sister Jennie at the rear. Lillian Beckwith cried and cried, she was so frightened, but she made her way bravely, holding the hands of the girls on either side.

Now we are all gathered here, waiting, waiting. Eight cows and two horses have been found and returned to the barn. The men and boys come in now and then to get warm. We have soup for them, and fresh-baked bread, and hot cider or cocoa to drink. The whole day is upside down, with no ringing of the bell for meals. The searchers come and go. We warm their coats and boots at the woodstoves. Beards and eyebrows are coated with ice, and their cheeks are crimson. There is no merriment, only worry and weariness.

A little while ago a cheer went up, suddenly. The two workhorses had found their own way back and appeared at the barn door. This is a heartening thing. But the men and boys wrestled themselves into their coats and boots and went back out again. There are many more animals still to save.

Later still. 7 p.m.

They are all in the barn! None of the animals have been lost! The last of them was brought in not thirty minutes ago, by Brother Delmer. We then had a meal together, after kneeling by our chairs and giving thanks. For the first time since I have been here, there were strangers in the dining room. Men and boys from the farms in the area had shown up to help throughout the long day, and we fed them all.

They came from miles away, some of them, urging their own horses through the blizzard because they knew we needed help.

We gave thanks for all of it, for the animals and their safety, for the world's strangers who helped us, for our warm dwelling and nourishing food, for the end of the snowstorm and the bright moon rising now over the lake.

And I gave thanks for something else. I didn't notice this at first. But Sister Jennie came to my chair and leaned down and whispered to me. When I looked, glancing over to where the weary men and boys sat silently eating, I saw it was true.

I bowed my head right there at the table, and murmured a thank-you to a Father-Mother God who looked, in my imagination, a little like Caroline and Walter Pierce. I expect that is sacrilegious and Mother Ann would be shocked. But it is what I saw, in that moment, when with a heart filled with relief and gratitude, I realized that Daniel had returned to Chosen Land.

Sunday, April 20, 1919

It is Easter.

The spring snow did not last. We can see grass again. Crocuses are up, and the lake is rippling with water. There is a breeze, and the willows bow and bend and sway.

At dinner we had Easter lily cakes. The girls who had been here last Easter had been telling the rest of us, the ones who are newer to Chosen Land, for months about the lily cakes. And they were not a disappointment. Beautiful, small, yellow and white cakes shaped and frosted to look like calla lilies. I wanted to save mine, not eat it, but it would have become stale. And of course there will be lily cakes again next Easter, and the one after that.

At every meal, I glance toward the men and boys, and there he is. Who knows what he went through during the months he was gone? Whatever it was, it changed him. He no longer looks angry. At school I look toward Daniel's desk, and there he is. One afternoon, when the boys were set to mathematics and were working hard on their papers, Sister Cora turned to the girls' side and pulled down a map, for Geography. With her wooden pointer, she pointed to a country in the center of South America. Without thinking, I blurted out, "Paraguay!"

I was right, and she commended me, and went on to talk about Paraguay's major products. I glanced over toward the boys and saw Daniel look my way with a big grin.

He attends to his schoolwork now, and after school he goes directly to the barn. I see him sometimes in the field, bringing the cattle up for their hay, and he walks with a different walk, no longer the stiff stride I remember.

After Easter dinner, since it was the Sabbath, I didn't run off to play with the other girls as I did yesterday. We each went our separate ways — to curl up with a book, or to take a quiet walk.

I found myself, all alone, making my way up the hill behind the orchard. I had gone there once in the fall with the other girls to play, and we had flung ourselves, rolling, down the hill in soft dried grass. Now the ground was still firm — not thawed yet, though the snow was gone — and the grass was brittle, but I could see new green shoots at its base. I climbed up past the herb garden and beyond the apple trees, to the place where I could look down at the village. There was the girls' shop, and the window of the retiring room that I share with Grace, Rebecca, and Polly. Behind it was the sisters' shop where I had helped with laundry and burned my fingers, ironing. The candy-making was also in the sisters' shop, and soon — soon, I hope — I will be helping there. Beside it, I could see the pale green willow tree with its sweeping branches. Behind the corner of the huge brick dwelling was the boys' shop, where Daniel lives, and beyond it the barn, where Elder William's dog lay napping in the open doorway.

I took it all in, thinking of everything that had brought me here — the sadness, the losses, the fear, the loneliness, and even the things that had left me shaking with anger. All of that was part of me, the me I had once been. But most of me now was at peace. Standing there, I remembered the words of one of my favorite Shaker songs.

'Tis the gift to be simple,
'tis the gift to be free,
'tis the gift to come down
where we ought to be,
and when we find ourselves in the place just right,
'twill be in the valley of love and delight.

From where I stood, I could see, suddenly, Grace and Rebecca walking along the road, each of them holding the hand of a little Beckwith girl. I took one more deep breath of the April air at the top of the hill. Then I started down to join my sisters.

EPILOGUE

With the other girls her age, Lydia moved as a teenager into the large brick dwelling and began to wear the Shaker dress.

She watched her brother, Daniel, graduate from high school at the one-room Shaker school, and three years later Lydia herself graduated at the top of her small class. The Shakers sent her to study and obtain her teaching credentials at the Normal School in Gorham, Maine. It was assumed that she would eventually teach in the school that she had attended. She assumed it, too. But in Gorham, Lydia glimpsed the world that she had left behind. Much of it felt unfamiliar to her. Gradually, though, she began to yearn for something she could not at first put a name to.

It was only when she met and grew to love a young biology professor named Ben Chamberlin that she understood the choice she would have to make. Returning to Chosen Land, she postponed signing the covenant. She talked to the eldresses and sisters, prayed for guidance, and eventually, not without sadness, left the Shaker life to marry when she was 23 years old. The Shakers gave her money — as they did for each one who chose to leave — to help her make a start in the world, and on the day she left Sabbathday Lake, Sister Jennie, with a hug, returned to her the opal ring that had been her grandmother's.

Lydia and Ben were married in 1930 at Woodfords Congregational Church in Portland. Eventually they had two daughters, whom they named Caroline and Lucy. In the years that followed, Lydia took her little girls occasionally to see the place where she had spent her early years. Noisy and giggling in the backseat, they always fell silent as the car turned onto the narrow road that separated the village, the same road Lydia had crossed each day to the schoolhouse. It was hard for them to imagine the quiet, orderly life that she had lived there. But they smiled shyly at the sisters who greeted her mother with such affection. One of them was Sister Jennie Mathers.

Daniel was fond of his shy, pretty nieces, but marriage and children never were part of his life. From school he moved comfortably into the daily life of a young Shaker man, and for many years was in charge of the farm animals and equipment at Chosen Land. He signed the covenant when he was 21 years old and lived his entire life quietly and humbly at Sabbathday Lake.

Lydia Pierce Chamberlin lived to be 83. She died in 1990, a widow by then, with six grand-children. For many, many years she had sent gifts at Christmas to the young girls at the Shaker community, calling each year to find out the number so that there would be an identical gift for each. The numbers gradually diminished, until finally there came a year when there were no more children at Sabbathday Lake. Older Shakers remained, though, as they do to this day.

LIKE THE
WILLOW
TREE

HISTORICAL NOTE

In early March 1918, a young soldier at a military base in Kansas reported to the infirmary. He had the flu. By the end of that day, over a hundred soldiers from the same base were also very ill.

These were the first reported cases of what became known as "Spanish influenza," one of the worst epidemics in this country. It spread quickly. Soldiers on their way to war carried it to France, and it began to move across Europe. Soldiers returning home arrived in Boston, and so did the flu. The first case in Massachusetts—a soldier at Fort Devens—was discovered on September 7th. A week later, the civilian population in Boston was affected. And on September 21st, 6,000 soldiers at Fort Devens were ill. In October, almost 200,000 Americans died.

The illness was fast and deadly, with symptoms of fever, hemorrhage, and pneumonia. A person who was well on Tuesday morning might feel ill by evening and be dead on Wednesday. In San Francisco, a hospital maternity ward held 42 new mothers. Nineteen of them died of the flu.

It made its way around the world and up to Maine that fall. There were not enough doctors, not enough medicine, not enough undertakers, not enough graves.

By the time the epidemic subsided after several months, there had been 675,000 deaths in the United States, much larger numbers than those who died in World War I. The actual worldwide mortality statistics are not known, but estimates range from 50 to 100 million deaths.

Many children, like the fictional Lydia and Daniel Pierce, were orphaned by the flu in 1918. The Pierce children, despite the tragedy that befell them, were fortunate in where they lived. Growing up in Portland, Maine, they were 27 miles from a place called Sabbathday Lake.

Two hundred years earlier, a small group of French religious radicals, exiled from southern France, arrived in London. In France they had been known derisively as *Les Trembleurs* (Shakers) because of their manner of worship, when a kind of trancelike ecstasy caused them to tremble and shout. In England they attracted few followers, but among those who did join them were former Quakers James and Jane Wardley. The deeply devoted Wardleys started a society of followers in Manchester, England, and in 1758 they were joined by a 22-year-old woman named Ann Lee.

Ann Lee, who would eventually profoundly affect the entire religious culture of the United States, was the uneducated daughter of a blacksmith. Always religious, she found herself increasingly inspired after she joined the Wardley Society. She began seeing visions and having revelations, and she preached so powerfully against sin that she aroused hostility and was persecuted, beaten, and briefly imprisoned. In 1774, she and eight followers, including the man she had married twelve years earlier (and with whom she had had four children, all of whom had died), traveled by ship to America and arrived safely in New

York after a dangerous voyage that took three months.

In America she separated herself from her husband. Her insights and revelations had begun to create what would be the founding precepts of her faith, and one of these was celibacy. Another was confession. Newer, later visions brought her to believe in communalism, pacifism, and equality of the sexes.

Gradually, her doctrine acquired converts in the new land. It did not happen quickly. The Declaration of Independence was signed and a war was fought and won. The small band of believers in the Shaker faith lived in a log cabin, women carefully separated from men, in the wilderness of upstate New York. In 1778, Eleanor Vedder became the first American convert.

In 1784, Ann Lee, now known as Mother Ann, died. She was only 48 but had been weakened by imprisonment and physical attacks over the years. Others assumed leadership of the church, which was based on her teachings, and began to acquire believers. Over the next few years, between 1790 and 1794, ten communities gathered together in New York and New England. The one at Sabbathday Lake, in Maine, was the last of these.

By 1800 there were about 1,375 Shakers. The religion moved westward, and in the next years, between 1806 and 1824, communities were formed in Ohio, Kentucky, and Indiana.

By 1819, there were 3,500 Shakers. In the 1840s, the religion reached its highest numbers, as much as 5,000. Because they were celibate, Shakers never reproduced. Their converts came from other faiths, and some were former slaves. In addition, they took in and cared for orphaned children, and many of these, on becoming adults, joined the faith in which they had been raised.

They lived what they believed in: lives of simplicity, equality, and hard work, following the teachings of Jesus and Mother Ann. They were industrious and innovative. They became famous for their inventions—the flat broom, the wooden clothespin, a double-chambered woodstove, the apple peeler, the circular saw, the washing machine — and for the meticulous quality of their furniture, clothing, baskets, and boxes.

The community at Sabbathday Lake, known by its spiritual name, Chosen Land, was always the smallest and poorest. But it remained even as other communities, their numbers diminishing, closed down. By 1900 there were only 800 Shakers left in America. In 2010, as I write this, there are only three.

At Sabbathday Lake, Brother William Dumont, who had become a Shaker at age nineteen, was appointed Elder ten years later, in 1880. At the same time, Sister Lizzie Noyes, who was then 35, became Eldress. Together they governed Chosen Land, working separately from each other but combining their business skills, religious devotion, and untiring energy to create a newly prosperous community.

It was into this community in 1918 that a fictional orphaned girl in a dirty dress arrived and was greeted by Sister Jennie Mathers. Sister Jennie was the caretaker for the younger girls in those years. Later, she would go on to other jobs within the community. She died in 1946 at the age of 68.

Elder William had died in 1930, at 78. Eldress Lizzie, 81, had died four years earlier.

Brother Delmer Wilson, who as a boy had refused to leave when his mother came for him, remained a Shaker all his life. He contributed enormously to the community. He created the steam-fitted greenhouse, built furniture, managed the orchards, and became such an accomplished photographer that he started a postcard industry. He was appointed Elder but refused to use the title. He died in 1961, when he was 88. Many of the existing photographs of Chosen Land and its Shakers were taken by Brother Delmer.

The Shaker songs that Lydia Pierce learned came from the many, many songs that I found in a collection published in 1884, called *Shaker Music*. The collected songs originated in many Shaker communities; I chose those with origins in Maine and New Hampshire.

Chosen Land had increased in size in 1931, when the Shaker community in Alfred, Maine, closed its doors and its 21 Shaker sisters moved to Sabbathday Lake. (One of them, Sister Minnie Greene, was the last remaining Shaker from Alfred when she died in 2001, at the age of 91.) But the community eventually, inevitably, grew smaller and smaller in number.

Several things conspired to bring change for the Shakers. In the eighteenth and nineteenth centuries, children in need in America were shuffled about in various, sometimes cruel, ways. In the 1700s they were often indentured to work. Orphanages, sometimes appalling institutions, existed in the nineteenth century. In the late 1800s, thousands of children were sent west on "orphan trains" in vague hopes that they would find a new life in new territory. Finally, in the early 1900s, the first state laws to prevent child abuse and neglect were enacted. Gradually our country's attention shifted to the protection of children, and with the Social Security Act of 1935, federal funding for child welfare increased. The foster care system began to evolve. No longer could an orphaned child be simply signed over to the Shakers.

During the same decades, more attention was being paid to the safety of the population in terms of food and medicine. For the previous century, the Shakers, with their thriving gardens, had earned much-needed income through the sale of medicinal herbs. At Sabbathday Lake, they had packaged and marketed something called "The Shaker Tamar Laxative." It consisted primarily of dried prunes and tamarinds, cassia bark, flavoring (sugar and wintergreen), and something called hyoscyamine, a powerful narcotic derived from the herb henbane. Tamar Laxative had been discontinued by the time Lydia Pierce arrived at Chosen Land because its popularity had decreased. But like the remedies sold by other Shaker communities, its end would have come with the passage of the Food and Drug Act in 1906, and federal acts that followed, which legally restricted the sale of drugs without extensive testing and precautions.

In this era, too, factory-made cloth was suddenly cheaper than Shaker-woven fabric. Times were changing, and something seemed to be coming to an end.

But at the same time as their membership decreased, there was a growing awareness of the historical importance of this quiet place in Maine. The Sabbathday Lake Shaker Village has now been designated a National Historic Site, and its assets have been placed in a public trust to ensure that the land and buildings will remain intact and unspoiled.

If you visit Chosen Land, come in summer. The fields are green, dotted with grazing sheep and Scottish Highlander longhorn cattle. The lake reflects the sky. The herb gardens are a profuse tangle of leaves and blossoms. Between Memorial Day and Labor Day, a guide will show you six of the eighteen buildings; the boys' shop where fictional Daniel Pierce lived is now a museum. The building where the visiting dentist once had his chair now houses the Shaker shop. The one-room school has become the Shaker Library, where scholars of all sorts come and go; and next door, behind its fence, is the silent cemetery with its single stone, carved SHAKERS, where Sister Jennie,

Elder William, Eldress Lizzie, Brother Delmer, and the many others all rest.

If you visit on a Sunday, you can attend the Sabbath service in the meeting house. It might be led by the three remaining Shakers: Brother Arnold Hadd, Sister Frances Carr, and Sister June Carpenter. As generations of Shakers have, they will read from the Old and New Testaments, lead the singing of the Shaker hymns, and invite testimony from the congregation.

During the other days of the week, they lead busy, productive lives largely indistinguishable from life in any rural community. They tend their animals, their gardens, their library, their kitchen, and their correspondence. They watch television in the evening — Sister June is an avid Red Sox fan — and enjoy visits from friends and relatives. They knit. They pray.

They still lead a Shaker life.

ABOUT THE AUTHOR

Lois Lowry is the acclaimed author of two Newbery Medal books, *Number the Stars* and *The Giver*. She has written many books for young readers, including *Gathering Blue*, *Messenger*, and the picture book *Crow Call*.

Buying a house in southwestern Maine and discovering the Sabbathday Lake community led her to develop the story that became Lydia Pierce's diary, *Like the Willow Tree*.

She notes, "Eight years ago, I bought a very old farmhouse in southwest Maine. It sits on a hilltop that had once been called Brigham Hill. I often found myself wondering what life was like in the late eighteenth century when the house was new. The granite foundation, the wide pine floors, the post-and-beam barn with its wooden pegs and hand-hewn nails—all of it felt saturated with memories of people who worked hard and, I hoped, had been happy here.

"Thirty miles away, by way of winding roads past lakes and small villages, I discovered a place that had come to life at almost the same time as Brigham Hill Farm. It was called Sabbathday Lake, and it was the site of a Shaker community.

"I had, some years before, visited the Shaker Village at Canterbury, New Hampshire, had had a tour, and been greeted pleasantly by elderly Sister Bertha Lindsay, one of the last living Shakers there. But she, I knew, had since died, and there were no longer any Shakers left at Canterbury.

"It was a surprise to find Sabbathday Lake and to discover that three Shakers remain in residence there — not feeble and pious, but busy, committed, and cheerful. On my first visit there, I joined a regular tour. Then, on a different day, I took the tour a second time. On several different days I simply walked around, absorbing the landscape and the history that seemed to permeate it. Finally I returned several times to ask questions of Brother Arnold Hadd, one of the three Shakers who still live in the dwelling there, and a knowledgeable historian. I used their library, read their journals and records, and imagined what I could not know. Then I created a little girl, gave her a name and a fictional life, and took her to Sabbathday Lake to live at Chosen Land."

— Lois Lowry, Bridgton, Maine